ALL OF YOU, ALWAYS

A WALKER BEACH ROMANCE

LINDSAY HARREL

For my precious mentor and friend, Roma Gavaza.
Your constant support and encouragement over the years have meant
more than you know, and I am blessed to call you family.

CHAPTER 1

So this was Walker Beach.

A place that would finally help Bella Moody assemble the puzzle of her past—*if* she did her job.

Bella angled her car down the Main Street loop. Flashes of the Pacific Ocean to her left reflected the sun's rays between the downtown buildings, which were painted in cheery yellows, robin blues, and coral pinks. Other than its location in California, Walker Beach was nothing like Bella's home in Los Angeles.

The town had character—she'd give it that. But despite the fact Mom had called the little tourist town a "summer hotspot," the streets didn't seem overly crowded, even on a Friday afternoon in July. Probably had something to do with the earthquake last weekend.

The earthquake that had finally given Moody Development an edge.

Before she could blink, Bella had cruised by an art gallery, City Hall, a bookstore, and a smattering of restaurants. After passing a small public parking lot, she hit the northern part of town, which finally showed evidence of the earthquake.

Bella slowed her car and rolled down her windows to take in

the damage, including a few downed roofs, some broken front windows, and siding that hadn't fared well against the force. From the reports she'd read, the tremor had only registered a 6.5 on the Richter scale, with no loss of lives but damage to several homes in the hills and about ten businesses along Main Street.

Including her destination—the Iridescent Inn.

She came to a crosswalk and stopped for a young pigtailed girl with a thirty-something couple. The girl turned to the adults and reached for them. "Mama! Daddy! Swing me!"

Laughing, they each took a hand and swung her between them as they crossed the road.

Bella rubbed a hand over her heart. That child didn't know how lucky she was. Not only to have a mom *and* a dad in her life but also to have the security of their love.

She rolled her windows back up. No sense in waxing sentimental about what had never been—at least for her. But the perfect picture in front of Bella reinforced her determination to find out what she'd always longed to know. Maybe even to change her future.

If only there were another way to obtain the information she sought.

Shaking loose of the grim thought, Bella hightailed it through the rest of town, past a huge community park situated along the beach, and about a mile outside of Walker Beach until she reached her destination. The Iridescent Inn sat on a bluff with a path that led down to a private beach.

Mom had chosen well. Now it was up to Bella to seal the deal.

She swallowed past her dry throat. Pulling into the parking lot, Bella climbed from her Lexus sedan. Only a single beat-up Ford pickup truck accompanied her car.

The breeze coming up from the ocean whipped Bella's brown ombre hair across her face as she maneuvered to her trunk and pulled a travel-sized suitcase from inside it. Bella headed toward the adorable inn. Of course, it was no Waldorf Astoria in Beverly Hills, but its Victorian-style wraparound porch and dormer windows cast it in the same cozy light as the rest of the town.

Bella's Louboutins crunched over the gravel parking lot as she approached the front door. From here, she couldn't make out any damage to the inn, but Mom's source had assured them that the hundred-year-old building hadn't escaped without a rather significant scratch. Bella reached for the knob on the red front door, but it held fast.

After knocking on the door without a reply, she whipped out her cell phone then looked up the inn's number and dialed. Her legs ached as she shifted from foot to foot, the result of being crammed into the car for nearly five hours—thank you, endless LA traffic.

Great. No answer.

The ground beneath her feet rumbled. Bella shoved her phone into her purse and held as steady as possible while riding out the aftershock, which only lasted thirty seconds. She would probably experience hundreds of little quakes while here.

A crash cracked through the air, and Bella's heart stuttered as she maneuvered into a defensive position despite the pencil skirt that restricted her movement. But other than a few cars passing on the street just beyond the inn, no one was anywhere to be seen. Bella turned her ear to the wind. Another collision, this one a bit quieter, came from the backside of the building, so she walked that way, suitcase in tow.

As she rounded the inn, she nearly gasped at the view—at the whiff of briny spray in the air that spoke of fun and relaxation in the sun. Of retreats and vacation. Of the West Coast at its finest.

No wonder Mom was willing to pay through the nose for this property. When combined with the two B&Bs that Moody

Development had already bought on either side of the Iridescent Inn, this location would make for a beautiful—and profitable—new resort.

Once Bella convinced Ben Baker to sell.

She let herself through the wrought-iron gate that led from a walled-in courtyard down toward the beach. Trees provided a lot of shade, and a stone fountain nearby gave a pleasant ambience despite the fact no water trickled down its face.

But that's where the charm gave way to destruction. From this side of the inn, the significant scratch—or scratches, rather—became obvious. The entire northwestern wing of the Iridescent Inn had visible damage, with a hole in the northern part of its roof, cracks in the western blue clapboard siding, and scattered roof tiles and wood that lay strewn below.

She walked closer, her eyes moving along the house, taking in every casualty. The poor old inn had met its match in the earthquake.

As she stood next to a partially collapsed winding staircase that led to a damaged upper-story deck, a pang of sympathy curled around Bella's heart—even though all this *was* to her advantage.

The ground began to shake again as nature showed off with another aftershock. A large dangling piece of the staircase's railing cracked and plummeted through the air toward Bella.

"Watch out!"

Before she could even shriek, a flash of movement crossed her path as someone knocked into her with a grunt, felling her breath. Bella rolled a few times until she landed on her back. Taking in a few gulps of air, she cringed at something beneath her and pulled out a sharp rock that she tossed aside.

"Are you hurt?"

Bella turned her head to find a man sitting next to her, groaning as he rubbed his head before looking her way.

She peered up into warm chocolate eyes and a handsome tan face. Her tongue grew heavy. "No."

Scratch that. Her knees and elbows pulsed with a raw pain like the first time she'd ridden a bike without training wheels at the age of seven. Down the hill she had flown, and when she'd reached the bottom, onto the asphalt she had splayed. As usual, Mom hadn't been there. "Nothing feels broken at least."

"That's good." The man peeled thick work gloves from his hands as he bent toward her, squinting, examining, his eyebrows knit together. "Your knees are scraped up, but it's nothing a good cleaning and some BAND-AIDs won't fix."

"Guess I won't be wearing my favorite little black dress anytime soon." Bella forced a chuckle at her bad joke. She wouldn't need to wear something fancy if she were here for any length of time.

Not that she intended to be—though if Mr. Baker turned out to be as obstinate toward Bella as he'd been toward Mom, well, who knew how long she'd be stuck in the middle of nowhere.

"Can you sit?" Her rescuer watched Bella, something deep and assessing in his gaze.

Bella's stomach roiled at the scrutiny as her mother's warning came to mind. *"You'll have to be on your toes at all times."*

Right. She needed to focus. This minor incident couldn't endanger her mission, however conflicted she was about it.

"I think so."

"Here. Let me help you." He offered his hand. His white long-sleeved T-shirt pulled against his broad chest.

"Thanks." Bella slipped her fingers inside his, nearly pulling away at the shock his touch rendered, like the static electricity that always clung to the end of a slide and zapped kids when they least expected it.

After getting her upright, the guy let go of her hand and ran his fingers through his blondish-brown crew cut. "I'm really sorry about this."

She glanced down at her injuries and nearly cried out. The heel of her left Louboutin pump had snapped off and laid lifeless on the dirty ground, a victim of the aftershock and subsequent fall. Mom had better reimburse that as a business expense.

"It's not your fault. I shouldn't have been standing so close to the staircase."

"I was out here cleaning up when I saw you." A yellow hard hat lay discarded upside down on the other side of him. Mr. Baker must have hired him to clear the debris from the earthquake damage. "Another second or two and that loose railing would have creamed you."

"Instead, you got the privilege." Her fingers clenched as the words she'd intended to be a joke released in a stiff tone.

He hesitated. "I was just trying to help."

"Oh, no. Yeah." Why were her words getting all jumbled in her delivery? She took a breath and tried again. "I'm grateful. Really."

"Well . . . I'll go fetch the first aid kit." Again the man studied her, almost as if he knew something about her.

I hope not. Shivering, Bella stood, wincing at an ache in her backside. "That's OK." She needed to get checked in, hopefully before meeting the inn's owner. First impressions were everything in Bella's world, and she was sure they mattered even outside of the big city. "I'll come with you." She located her suitcase a few feet away.

His eyes narrowed for a moment. "Are you . . ." He massaged his jaw for a moment then shook his head and headed toward the front of the hotel.

Well, that was strange. She followed him, hobbling on her broken heel.

He snuck a hand into the pockets of his Dickies and emerged with a key that he used to open the door before pushing his way inside. Huh. Maybe he was more than a contractor hired to fix the earthquake damage.

The inside of the inn exuded just as much charm as the outside, and from here Bella wouldn't have even known of the damage along its northwestern facade. Real wood floors led to a quaint reception desk that welcomed guests into the ten-by-ten foyer. Behind it, a staircase ascended to a second level. If memory served from her brief moments perusing the website, the twenty-room inn had a small lobby at the top of the stairs and rooms on both floors. The deck she'd seen from the courtyard in the back met up with the lobby and provided guests with a gorgeous view of the ocean and beach below.

Speaking of other guests, where were they?

Bella cleared her throat. "I'm guessing all that debris is from the earthquake?"

"Yeah, and things are a mess. Most of the town was spared, but a few of us were hit hard. It could have been worse." The workman squatted behind the reception desk and started digging, finally emerging with a box of bandages and a tube of what she assumed was antibiotic ointment.

"Here you go." He shoved the stuff into her hands and leaned back against the desk, chiseled arms folded over his chest. The scent of clean soap lingered in the space between them.

"Thanks." The edges of the BAND-AID wrappers crinkled in her fingers. She itched to get out of her dusty clothes, but this was a prime opportunity to gather intel. And even though her assignment left a sour taste in her mouth, that's why she was here after all. "Were there any guests staying at the inn when the earthquake struck?"

Something ticked in the man's jaw. "Thankfully not." His arms tightened, emphasizing his biceps even more. "Speaking of guests, I notice you have a suitcase with you, but I don't have any reservations in my system for today. Can I ask what you were doing in my courtyard?"

His system? *His* courtyard? Bella blinked. "Are you the owner?"

"Yep. Ben Baker, at your service."

"Oh." She couldn't hold back her grimace. So much for first impressions. "Nice to meet you."

"And you are?"

She couldn't miss how steel rimmed his tone. Something about his clear distrust weakened her muscles. But why should she care what he thought? She didn't know him. And Bella Moody was used to playing ball with much more intimidating businessmen than Ben Baker.

Of course, in this case, playing ball meant using stealth. Getting the inside scoop. Winning him over so she could discover his weaknesses and take what she wanted.

Well, what Mom wanted.

But if Bella succeeded, her mother would finally give Bella what *she* wanted. The one thing she wanted more than anything. The thing *only* Mom could give.

Information.

She stepped forward, her legs wobbly—and not just because of her missing heel. Guess she cared what he thought after all.

"Bella M—" Yikes, she'd almost ruined everything with one word. She needed to stick with her plan if things weren't going to fall apart in the first five minutes. More than they already had, anyway. "Bella Miranda."

At least she wasn't lying. Miranda was her middle name.

It was a small consolation.

Stay focused. Remember why you're really here. Let that guide you.

"And what are you doing in town?"

"I'm here on a personal errand." She glanced at her suitcase. "And no, I don't have a reservation, but I was hoping you'd have space for me."

He lifted off the desk, his arms falling to his sides. "You

really want to stay here after nearly being taken out by that railing?"

"Is it safe on the inside?" If not, she'd have to find somewhere else in town to stay, some other way to get to know Ben. The whole plan would go much more smoothly if she could be here.

"The building inspector finally came today and gave me the all-clear to enter. Only half of the inn is damaged. If you stay away from the courtyard and don't go north of the lobby, you should be OK." The pinched look on his face relayed his resignation. "But I'd need you to sign a waiver stating that you understand the risks."

"All right."

He waited for a beat. "All right as in . . ."

"I'll stay."

Was that a kindling of hope smoldering in Ben's eyes? It was there and gone so quickly that maybe she'd imagined it. "We do, in fact, have a few vacancies right now." He rounded the desk and snagged the computer mouse. "Do you want one queen or two twins?"

"One queen is fine."

"And how long do you want to stay?"

"Can we just start with a week? I'll let you know if I need to stay longer."

Ben glanced up. "You don't know how long you'll be here?"

"I'm not sure when my business will be concluded." And wasn't that the truth? "One more thing. I'd like to pay in cash, if that's all right."

Ben's eyebrows lifted. "We normally require a credit card on file in case there are damages."

She couldn't give him a credit card with her real last name on it, now could she? Her stomach twisted at the need for such deceit, but she pushed the uneasiness aside. "I'm happy to pay for a week at a time up-front, plus I can give you a deposit in case there are damages. Not that I plan to damage anything."

He studied her for a moment, probably weighing whether she'd walk out if he refused. Finally, he nodded. "You're not the first person to come to Walker Beach looking for anonymity. Two hundred should cover the deposit, which will be refunded when you check out as long as nothing's damaged."

"Sounds great."

He took her cash then worked to check her in.

So far, except for his penetrating gazes and slightly bristly manner, he'd been all business—an admirable quality, actually, considering how often guys hit on Bella when she was doing the most mundane of tasks like grocery shopping or working out at the gym. But this was one instance where a chatty demeanor would have been helpful.

Because everything was riding on getting Ben to like her.

And people didn't open up to those they didn't like, so to succeed here, she needed to gain his trust. At least, that's what Mom had said before she'd sent Bella off on this mission.

Hating herself more than a little and feeling as fake as a metal tree at Christmas, Bella cocked a hip and propped an arm on the desk. While Ben clicked around on the screen, she pointed to a framed photo a few inches away that showed a huge group of people smiling at the camera. "Is that your family?"

Not looking up, he nodded. "Yep. Family reunion last year."

She peered closer and finally found Ben in the upper left corner, his arm slung around a tall blond girl with similar features. "Who's that?"

He looked up with a frown and something like irritation in his eyes. "My sister, Ashley."

What would it be like to have a real family—not just a mom who was more a boss than anything?

Maybe, at the end of all this, Bella would finally know.

Keep him talking. Right. "So, what's there to do around here?"

A printer whirred to life behind Ben. He snagged some papers and turned, handing them to Bella along with a pen. "Tons. Of course, there's surfing, kayaking, and other water sports. If you need any equipment or want to take a tour, my cousin Cameron manages a rental shop and could set up something for you. There's also a lot of shopping downtown if antiques, art galleries, and specialty shops are your thing."

She flourished her signature across the safety waiver and contract detailing the security deposit regulations. "Any good places to eat?"

"My personal favorites are Froggies Pizza and the Frosted Cake."

Her stomach rumbled to life at the suggestions. The tiny pack of airplane peanuts she'd found at the bottom of her purse hardly sufficed for a meal, but that's all she'd eaten since breakfast. "Those sound amazing." She angled her head and pushed her lips into a grin that felt anything but natural. "Would you happen to be available to join me?"

Ben stiffened. "Can't. The earthquake put me behind on everything."

Great. The prickly owner clearly wanted nothing to do with her—except to take her money, of course. What now? "Rain check, maybe?"

"I'm really slammed." He averted his eyes and slid a key card against the desk's polished surface. "Your room is just upstairs and down the south hallway. Third door on the left. If you need anything, I'll be in my office, which is just around the corner off the kitchen."

Bella snatched the key card and tried for a casual tone. "Sounds good. Thanks."

She strode toward the staircase, wincing at the tightened skin on her kneecaps. Maybe this *was* more like that first time riding a bike than she'd realized, with the hill too steep and Bella too bullheaded to see she shouldn't attempt it.

But just like that day twenty years ago, she was going to keep dragging her bike all the way to the top. She was going to have to change her strategy, but she'd try again and again until she finally mastered it.

No matter her own reservations, she *would* get Ben Baker to agree to sell his inn to her mom. It didn't matter that Mom had been trying for at least six months. Bella could accomplish what no one else could simply because she had more riding on this than anyone else.

Sure, Mom wanted the deal so she could finally build the resort she'd been dreaming of. The place would be a gold mine.

But Bella wanted something more than money. She and her mom had come from poverty, and poverty could find them again at any time. But a family—well, families were forever. And Bella wanted to know if she had one out there, somewhere.

So, bring on the hill because Bella Moody would do just about anything to find out who her father was and whether he'd been survived by any family when he'd died twenty-seven years ago.

Numbers were Ben Baker's enemy.

Especially when they were red. Very, very red.

Ben scrubbed a hand across his face and leaned back in his office chair as the spreadsheet swam in front of him on the screen. Grandpa would roll over in his grave if he could see how badly Ben was botching his legacy.

His one saving grace would be the insurance money from the earthquake, which he hoped he would get an update on by Monday. He'd likely have to do most of the repairs himself—and maybe he'd snag his buddy Evan or a few of his cousins to help out—but that would leave extra money on the table to pay off some of his debts.

Like the mortgage he'd defaulted on three months ago.

But if the four cancellations that had just come in this afternoon and the numbers bleeding on the screen indicated what was to come, the Iridescent Inn was in dire trouble.

Ugh. He needed a break.

Easing away from the desk, Ben strode to his office door then into the hallway and up the stairs toward the lobby, where the world's most comfortable couches awaited him. Maybe a little time stretched out on one of those bad boys would refresh him enough to come up with a plan.

But as he reached the top of the stairs and pivoted toward the pair of deep green couches ringing the stone fireplace against the south wall, Ben halted.

There sat the woman who had checked in only a few hours ago, a large pizza box on the scratched oak coffee table in front of her along with a stack of plates and napkins. She glanced up at his arrival. "Oh. Hi. I hope it's OK I'm in here."

Earlier she'd been all business in that skirt that had hugged her curvy lower half and heels that had looked painful to walk in. Now she looked much more relaxed—though somehow still classy—in black yoga pants and a flowy blue shirt that brought out the chocolate brown of her eyes.

The same eyes that had drawn him in earlier when he'd "rescued" her in the courtyard. Ben had imagined something mysterious and vulnerable in their depths. Probably he'd just whacked his head harder than he'd thought.

"Of course it's OK." His voice came out gruffer than he'd intended. He attempted to soften his tone. "I didn't mean to intrude."

"You're not. I was just thinking it would be nice to have some company. And there's plenty of food." The woman—Bella, if he remembered correctly—waved her hand toward the Froggies pizza box. Even from here the smell of hot cheese and his uncle's secret pizza sauce tantalized his senses. "Would you like to join me?"

"Thanks for the offer, but I have a ton of work to do." He really did but that wasn't his prime motivation for turning her down. "And I'm not hungry." Neither was that.

His stomach chose that moment to betray him. It rumbled like a train coming into the station.

The woman quirked an eyebrow. "Of course you're not."

When she opened the lid of the box, Ben couldn't help but lean forward at the sight of pepperoni and sausage spread generously across the top of the pizza. "I guess I'll have some." He reached into his back pocket, snagged his wallet, and pulled out a ten, which he tossed next to her onto the couch. "That should cover my half."

"Not necessary. It's my treat." Bella took a piece of pizza from the box, slid it onto a plate, and held it out for Ben. "Here."

Ben accepted the plate then shifted on his feet. "Thanks. But seriously, keep the money." On the off chance she was trying to make this into some sort of date, maybe his insistence would make it clear he was not interested. "I should go back to my office."

Bella settled back against the couch. "I understand." Her tone remained crisp, professional. "Hope you get a lot done." Moving her gaze to the unlit fireplace, she bit into the pizza and chewed.

Aw, man. Something about the interaction wasn't sitting right with him. His mom's voice yapping at him to treat women well—dumb chivalry—resounded in his mind, and it seemed wrong to leave Bella to eat here alone in a town where she might not know anyone.

And all because he was, what? Afraid she was flirting with him? Most likely she was just a nice person and offering a hungry guy some food.

Not all women were conniving like Elena.

Besides, he didn't want to insult the one paying customer willing to stay in an inn falling down around her ears. "All right. I can stay for a few minutes." Then he'd get out of there and back to the safety of his office. Ben slid onto the other couch and bit into the pizza but didn't taste a thing.

The clock on the mantel ticked. Loudly.

After several minutes of silence, Bella finished her pizza. Once she'd placed the plate on the coffee table, she wiped her lips with a napkin. "That was really good. Thanks for the recommendation."

Maybe she'd go back to her room now.

But nope. She stayed put.

Ben suppressed a sigh. "I'll pass along the compliment to my uncle and aunt. Froggies is their restaurant."

"Please do. I think I met another Baker when I was out, just before I grabbed the pizza. The owner of Serene Art? Any relation?"

"My aunt Jules."

Bella crossed her legs. "Your aunt? She looked really young."

"She's forty-two." Only ten years older than him. His first babysitter.

"It sounds like you have a lot of family in town."

"Yeah. My dad has four siblings, and they're all here."

She tilted her head. "Are all of them business owners?"

"Yep."

"Wait, seriously?"

Was her response disbelief or awe? Or maybe a mix of both. So strange because it was just Ben's reality and always had been. "My dad owns Walker Beach Construction. Froggies is my Uncle Thomas's. Aunt Kiki owns the antique store on Main. And Aunt Louise runs a shop that sells fancy oils and vinegars."

He nearly gagged as the words tumbled out. Since when did he tell strangers his family history? Ben stuffed the rest of his slice into his mouth.

"Oil Me This, right? I stopped in there and bought some smoky bacon olive oil."

"Mmhmm." He swallowed. How could he end their conversation without seeming rude?

Bella stood and walked to one of the old brown bookcases flanking the fireplace then squatted next to a stack of board games. "And did I see that the beach and that large community park on the water are named after your family?"

Maybe one-word answers would kill her inquiries. "Yeah."

She glanced back at him, eyes wide. "Is the entire town run by the Baker clan?"

"We were just one of the founding families." The way her mouth hung open was kind of comical. Ben couldn't help but chuckle. "OK, the biggest founding family. I have eleven first cousins on the Baker side, and that doesn't even include all of the cousins on my great-aunt's side—the Griffins. Almost all of them live in town."

"That's intense." Bella pulled a red box from the bookcase. "Where does this inn come in? Is it part of the Baker family legacy too?" She wandered back to the couches and sat with Yahtzee in her hands. What did she plan to do with that? Didn't she know the game required more than one player?

He scratched behind his ear. "My great-great-grandparents originally built the inn."

"That must be nice—to be part of something bigger than yourself." Bella's voice was almost wistful as she cleared a spot on the coffee table then opened the lid of the box. She placed two pads of paper, pens, a plastic cup, and five dice on the table.

Guess he'd been wrong about her not knowing anyone here. Bella was expecting company.

Instead of relief, a hollow ache pinched Ben's chest.

What was he *doing*? He couldn't afford to get distracted by a pretty face. Not again. The inn was too important, and he'd already allowed his grief to overshadow his responsibilities for the last seven months.

Here, at least, was a clear chance for him to escape. Ben cleared his throat. "I guess. It's a lot of work. And I probably should get back to it."

Bella eyed him. "You up for a game first?"

"Oh. I—"

"Unless you're afraid to lose. This was my favorite game when I was a kid, and I warn you—I am good." She smiled in challenge. The gesture softened the edges of her businesslike aura, making her a bit more . . . approachable.

Definitely more beautiful, if that were possible.

Danger, danger, Will Robinson. "I really shouldn't."

"Right. Sorry. I don't want to stop you from doing your work. Believe me, I understand having a busy schedule." Bella worried her lip and there—another flash of the vulnerability he'd glimpsed earlier in her eyes.

Was she playing him? Trying to manipulate him? Or actually disappointed he wasn't staying? Ben couldn't trust himself to tell anymore.

Curse you, Elena.

Probably he should give Bella the benefit of the doubt. At the very least, he should be a gracious host. "No, no. I'd love to play." Fine, *love to* was a reach. A big one.

"You sure? Really, I don't want to keep you." The sincerity in her tone rang true. At least, he thought so.

He groaned inwardly at the seesaw in his mind. "I'm sure."

"Awesome. You know the rules?"

"Yep."

Bella placed the dice in the cup and held it out toward him. "Ladies first."

A hint of another smile graced her lips before she shook the cup then tipped it. Dice spilled onto the table. Gathering three of them, she dropped the dice into the cup and rolled again. "I can't help noticing that you don't sound too happy about owning the inn."

Was she a mind reader? Or maybe a lawyer. That would explain the fancy getup from earlier and her ability to trick him into spilling his guts. "No. It's great. Just a lot of pressure." Pressure he was caving under.

Bella recorded her play on her paper pad and passed him the cup of dice. "So why not sell?"

He scoffed at her casual question. "Yeah, right."

"Why not?"

Ben shook and rolled the dice, snagging three fours, a six, and a one. He collected the last two and rerolled them. "My family has owned the inn for just about a hundred years. They built it from the ground up. I couldn't sell it even if I wanted to."

And some days, he did. He'd never planned to inherit it, had always figured he'd keep working for his dad's construction company like he'd been doing since he was sixteen. Maybe, eventually, partner with him.

But seven months ago Grandpa died, and Grandma signed over the inn to her eldest grandchild. She'd said it was too much for her "old bones" and that maybe he could infuse new life into the place.

And here he was, leading it toward an early grave.

He knew Grandma had probably just pitied him, was trying to give him something to focus on instead of how he'd been embarrassed and betrayed in front of the entire town two months before that. But he hadn't had the heart to tell her he wasn't ready to own a business, especially one he knew next to nothing about.

Bella glanced at his dice. "Four fours. Nice!" Then she looked back at him and shrugged. "Surely your family would understand. It's your life, after all." Her eyes caught his, and for a moment his insides buzzed around the edges—a foreign feeling he couldn't quite define. "This is a beautiful property. You must have received offers at some point."

He picked up the final dice, tossed it into the cup. It rattled around inside. "A few."

"Did you consider them?"

He let the dice fly across the table, hoping to see a four. Wouldn't he end the game by rolling a Yahtzee? It had been a while since he'd played.

A three stared up at him. So close.

Ben sighed. "For about a minute. But I can't in good faith sell. It's not just about me."

"What do you mean?"

"Look, this is Walker Beach. My home. I've lived here my entire life. Unlike the two idiots who used to own the properties on either side of me, I'm not selling to some money-grubbing real estate developer whose main goal is to ruin my town."

Bella flinched. And for good reason—he'd practically shouted the words. Oops.

"How would selling your inn ruin the town?" Bella collected the dice off the table. "It's not like you're running a vibrant business that's contributing massively to the economy."

Wow. "Way to shoot a guy in the heart."

Bella fumbled the dice onto the floor. "Sorry." She grimaced. "I shouldn't have said that. This place, its history, means a lot to you."

"It does." And a city girl like her couldn't possibly get it. "If I sell to the highest bidder, what is a peaceful vacation destination will become overrun with tourists who don't appreciate what makes Walker Beach special."

"And what is that?" She straightened in her seat.

"We're an artsy community with some unique shops and restaurants, but it's more than that." He really shouldn't have to justify himself to this stranger. But for some inexplicable reason, he wanted her to understand. "I guess, for me, it's just . .

. everyone here is family, whether you're related or not. Folks care about each other and help each other. You can't find that in the big city or even in every small town you visit."

Bella leaned forward, hands folded over her stomach, wincing. Once again, he'd let his forceful tone loose. Some gracious host he was turning out to be.

"Sorry. You hit on a sore subject."

Without either of them officially ending the game, Bella began to put it away. "No, I'm sorry. I didn't mean . . . didn't realize . . ." She looked up at him, cheeks red.

Great. He'd embarrassed her. "It's fine."

"It's not." The game packed, she closed the pizza box and stood. "Thanks for the pizza and the game, but I'll leave you in peace now. Good night, Ben."

Then she turned on her heel and was gone.

Lying back on the couch, he rubbed his face and stared at the stark white popcorn ceiling. Peace? Ha. It seemed like Ben would never find peace again.

Guys failing miserably were bound to live in turmoil.

CHAPTER 2

*I*t was a gorgeous day.

Too bad that instead of enjoying it, Bella would be doing recon on Ben Baker.

Baker Beach's warm sand sifted between her toes as she walked south from the inn. Bella's ears reverberated with the ocean's roar, her constant companion for the last mile she'd walked from the Iridescent Inn toward town.

The beach south of Ben's and Moody Development's properties became part of the six-acre Baker Community Park—a pleasant scene that, at noon on a Saturday, was already crowded with families cooking in the barbecue pits, kids running around in the grassy playground area, and beachgoers lounging with umbrellas and chairs in the sand.

The song from the latest Broadway musical blasted from Bella's back pocket. Even though she felt more powerful when dressed in her business outfits, Walker Beach required a more casual touch, so today she'd opted for her Lucky white jean shorts and a sleeveless black tunic.

She snatched the phone and checked the caller ID. "Hey, Jess."

"So, what's up with this text you sent me yesterday? I can't believe you're bailing on our girls' night."

"I know, I'm sorry. Like I said, something came up last minute."

"A work-something or a mom-something?"

"Aren't they one and the same?" Being Bella's best friend since grade school meant Jessica Morales knew the ins and outs of Bella's complicated relationship with Mom.

A beach ball floated toward Bella from a group of teens who'd been hitting it back and forth. "You know I wouldn't back out of girls' night for just anything, though." Using her fist, she bumped the ball back to the teens, who waved to thank her.

"I should hope not." Her friend's teasing tone came through the phone.

Bella rolled her eyes. "Please. You've missed girls' night more than once for a hot date."

"Is that what you have?" Jess's voice shot up a notch. "A hot date?"

The memory of Ben Baker, all muscle and sculpted jaw, flashed in Bella's mind. She promptly dismissed it. "Of course not. I'm in Walker Beach, and I don't know how long I'll be here."

"Where's that?"

"It's a little tourist town off Highway 1 between LA and San Fran."

"Wait, so you went on a weekend vacay and didn't invite your best friend?"

Bella trudged through the sand, her leg muscles burning with the constant motion of sinking then pulling out her feet. "I told you. It's a work thing." She gave Jessica the basic details of why she was there. "If I can get this guy to sell his property to Mom, then Mom will tell me everything she knows about my dad."

If only it were that simple.

"This is Walker Beach. My home. I'm not selling to some money-grubbing real estate developer whose main goal is to ruin my town." Ben's words from last night pummeled her like the waves beating the shore a few feet away.

"So, was this thing her idea or yours?"

Ah, there was the rub. If only Bella could blame it entirely on Mom. "Both. I was in her office when she got a call from one of the VPs about the need to secure this property soon." Bella swiped a drop of sweat from her forehead as she maneuvered around some children digging holes in the sand. "Mom suggested maybe I could succeed where she failed because I was, quote, 'pretty and good at getting what I want.'"

"Sounds like her. What did you say?"

"I said no way. But then Mom said she'd give me anything I wanted. A promotion? Done. A raise? It would be mine."

"And you asked for the one thing you knew she'd never give unless she was desperate."

"You make it sound so cold and calculating." Bella's sunglasses may have muted the bright colors of the umbrellas dotting the beach, yet a headache was forming behind her eyes anyway. "But after this, I may actually know more about my dad than his first name and that he died when I was a baby."

Couldn't Jess understand what was driving Bella? But no, how could she? She had an amazing family, one that Bella had come to know well thanks to countless weeknight dinners and weekend sleepovers as they'd grown up together.

Jessica's silence chafed like the sand one of the kids flung against her leg as Bella passed. Finally, her friend spoke. "Bells, come on. Lying to some guy you don't know? That's not you."

Yeah. Jess definitely didn't understand. "I'll take that under advisement." After a terse goodbye, Bella hung up the phone then pulled up directions for her destination.

The Frosted Cake, a supposed local favorite, should be a great place to overhear the latest town gossip. If the directions on her phone were correct, it would take only a few minutes to reach the South Village restaurant Ben had mentioned yesterday.

Bella veered toward the edge of Baker Park and onto the board-walk that ran the length of the town. And then, without the conver-sation with Jessica to distract her, the memory of last evening, of time spent in Ben Baker's presence, rose sharp in Bella's mind.

She had definitely sensed him walking on eggshells—the tight jaw, the scrunched brow, the pursed lips. At first, anyway. After a while he'd loosened up a tad. She'd almost felt like they were getting somewhere. When he'd agreed to stay for the game, Bella had nearly fallen off the couch.

Then it had all unraveled. The way he'd described his town, his family, his people had resonated so deeply inside of her. Because he had what Bella had always wanted. And according to him, her success meant his loss.

She'd had to get out of there quickly before she did some-thing foolish like cry. Because Jess was right about one thing—this wasn't her. She was much more comfortable in a board-room, giving a presentation, or working a budget than cozying up to a stranger, even if said stranger was extremely attractive.

But her friend was wrong too. Bella had promised herself at the beginning that she absolutely would not lie. Even though this had been Mom's idea, Bella didn't have to adopt her tactics. And so far, she hadn't said one untrue thing.

Still, the faster she learned what she needed to know, the faster she could accomplish her task and get away from Ben Baker and Walker Beach—and the things they made her feel.

The GPS on her phone told her to turn left off the board-walk, so Bella took the connected sidewalk that led to Main Street and found the Frosted Cake. Upon entering the diner-slash-bakery, warmth and the heavenly smell of cooked beef and chocolate engulfed her. The place wasn't huge, but there were several occupied tables toward the back and a to-go counter with a line several people deep.

A pastry case next to the counter displayed an assortment of desserts that set Bella's mouth watering, especially the devil's food cake. Several groups of people lingered in the tiny entrance lobby, presumably waiting to be seated. Everyone looked like they knew someone else.

Like they knew exactly where they belonged.

Now what? How was Bella supposed to get information, especially with no tables available? Suddenly her plan to "meet people" and "listen in" to gossip sounded short-sighted and out of her depth.

Sure, she was good at schmoozing with other company executives at a mixer or gala, but this was different. Half the people here were in bathing suits and cover-ups, and most of them talked with an ease and openness that Bella hardly recognized. The jovial woman with white hair behind the counter seemed to know everyone who walked in the door. And maybe, except for Bella, she really did.

The bell jangled behind her, and Bella turned. No way. It really *was* a small world. Or a small town, anyway. Because there stood Ben's sister, Ashley. The woman looked just like her photo, with sculpted shoulders and the look of a tall, sleek runner. She was accompanied by a shorter leggy blonde with kind eyes.

The women headed for the to-go line, and Bella followed. Being a creepy stalker wasn't exactly what she'd signed up for. But she just needed an in, a way to jump into the conversation without freaking out Ben's sister.

Pretending to study the menu behind the counter, she listened to the women's conversation. For a few minutes they chatted about work and some upcoming wedding between a family member named Tyler and his fiancée Gabrielle.

They were nearing the front of the line. This was never going to work.

"—and the inn looks terrible. I hope Ben hears about the insurance money soon."

Bingo.

Inhaling a deep breath, Bella tapped Ashley on the shoulder. "Excuse me."

Ashley turned. "Hi." Cocking her head, she smiled.

Huh. Not how most women in LA would have reacted to someone interrupting them.

"Hi." Bella forced herself to return the grin despite the nausea roiling in her stomach. "I'm really sorry to butt in, but are you talking about the Iridescent Inn?"

"We were." Ashley's brow crinkled.

Yeah, Bella sounded like a major snoop. She rushed on. "I'm staying there. It's a beautiful property."

"It really is." The smile was back. There was something altogether too welcoming and friendly in Ashley's posture. In this whole place, really. "I'm Ashley. The owner Ben is my brother. Oh, and this is my cousin, Shannon."

"I'm Bella." Bella turned to the demure woman beside the more gregarious cousin. Shannon's hair fell past her shoulders in waves. Between her high cheekbones, large round eyes, and small nose and chin, hers was a babydoll face. Like her cousin, she was thin, though a bit less muscular. "Ben mentioned having a lot of cousins."

"Yeah, we're a big family."

Ashley tossed her hair over her shoulder. "So, Bella, are you visiting family here? Maybe we know them."

"No. I don't know anyone here." She paused, her brain racing to fill in the silence so Ashley wouldn't follow up with any other questions about what Bella was doing in Walker Beach. "That's why it was so nice of Ben to join me for dinner last night."

Shannon coughed. "I'm sorry, did you say dinner?"

"How did that come about?" Ashley's eyebrows formed a V.

What was with their reaction? She stuffed her hands into her back pockets. "I was in the lobby with a pizza, and he came in, so I asked him if he wanted some and . . ." Bella shrugged. "He stayed for a bit."

"Next." The woman behind the counter greeted them. The line had moved faster than Bella had thought it would. Great. Not much time left to get to know Ashley and Shannon.

"Hey, Ms. Josephine." Ashley stepped forward. "I've got a call-in order under my name. And you can add on whatever she's having." She hooked a thumb toward Bella.

What? No. "That's not necessary."

"I wouldn't argue with her, hon." Ms. Josephine winked, her eyes twinkling. "What'll it be?"

"Oh. Um." Her eyes flitted back to the menu. "The turkey club, please."

"Coming right up." She called out the order to her kitchen staff then swiped Ashley's credit card.

The three women stepped aside so the next customers could order. Bella tugged at the strap of her purse. "Thanks. You didn't have to do that." *I really wish you hadn't.*

"It's no biggie." Ashley shrugged. "We take care of people here."

Where was she, Mayberry? "Well, thank you again."

"Of course." Ashley tucked her credit card into her wallet, which she dropped into a blue messenger bag. "Would you like to join us for lunch on the beach?"

Bella couldn't have asked for a better opportunity than that to fall into her lap. Yet her tongue stuck to the top of her mouth as she pushed out her answer. "Sure."

They chatted for a few minutes. Ashley was an events coordinator and Shannon a preschool teacher, and both had lived in Walker Beach their entire lives. Bella found herself nearly forgetting why she was here.

"Order up, Ashley Baker!" Ms. Josephine slid a bag of food across the counter. "You ladies have a nice day."

Thanking her, Ashley snagged the bag. They headed outside, stepping onto the sidewalk that led between the buildings and met up with the boardwalk just beyond. Once they found an empty spot on the fairly crowded beach, they sat.

Ashley unpacked the bag and handed out the items inside. "So, if you don't know anyone here, what brings you to Walker Beach, Bella? You vacationing?"

Ugh. The dreaded question.

Bella took a quick bite to keep from answering right away, and the delicious blend of turkey, bacon, ham, Swiss, and some sort of tangy raspberry chipotle spread distracted her for a few moments.

How to answer Ashley's question?

Just tell the truth. As much as you can, anyway.

"No, not vacationing." She paused. "I'm here because I want to find my dad."

Shannon lowered her sandwich and placed a hand on Bella's arm. The touch and her expression were so genuine that heat pricked the back of Bella's eyes.

"Sounds like there's a story there." Ashley clearly didn't want to pry, but she'd said the perfect thing, in the perfect way, to invite more conversation if Bella wanted to share.

Whoa. OK, this recon mission was quickly going south. She wasn't here to make friends. Yet she'd made some anyway, without trying.

Bella bit into her sandwich again and looked out across the ocean. The waves lapped against the shore that had been invaded by toddlers and flirting teens and adults. But they never stopped going in and out. Despite their surroundings, the waves remained strong, undeterred, constant.

Just like Bella needed to be.

She returned her attention to Ashley and Shannon, who

were watching her. "Why were you guys so surprised that Ben would eat dinner with me? Should I feel insulted?" She smiled to let them know she was joking, but Shannon's cheeks reddened.

"That's not what we meant at all."

"Definitely not." Ashley bit her lip. "My brother has been . . . well, not himself for the last nine months."

"Why's that?" Bella leaned in. She wanted to know the answers—and not merely for recon purposes.

Whoa, what? No, no, no. She could not develop feelings of any sort for Ben Baker, romantic or otherwise. Emotions clouded judgment, and she had to stay focused. Besides, the two of them had nothing in common. And he had seemed just to tolerate her presence.

The cousins exchanged a glance before Ashley spoke again. "Last October he was supposed to get married, but his fiancée ran away with an attorney from Seattle who was staying at the inn. She left a note in her bridal suite the morning of the wedding."

Oh no. Poor Ben. No wonder he'd been so standoffish, so reticent to join her for dinner. He'd probably thought she was hitting on him. She held back a groan.

"That's terrible." Bella couldn't imagine the heartache. Her most serious relationship had occurred during her senior year of high school, and she'd only casually dated since then. Sure, Jake had broken her seventeen-year-old heart, but at least she hadn't been left at the altar.

Still, just enough of the bitterness remained that if Ben's ex were standing in front of her she might have wanted . . . well, she didn't know what, but it wouldn't have been pretty.

Bella finished her sandwich. Ack. She swallowed around the sharp taste of onion that overtook the last bite as she tried to shove down her emotions.

You have a job to do. Don't forget it.

Drawing another breath, Bella tried to ignore the sinking feeling that walking through this door would be a mistake. But how could it be a mistake if it led to her discovering more about her father?

Even these two women would understand that. After just a half-hour spent in their presence, it was clear that family meant everything to them.

And Bella wanted a family more than anything.

Bella forced her body to relax and smiled past the uncertainty. "So, is your whole family close?"

CHAPTER 3

*H*e was the biggest idiot in California.

"The insurance agent called and told me the news this morning." Ben tossed another pile of debris into the renovation dumpster he'd rented Saturday and turned to his friend Evan Walsh, who'd traded in his Monday work slacks and nice button-up shirt for thick pants, a T-shirt, and brown gloves. "I don't even remember refusing earthquake insurance when it was offered. What kind of California business owner would do that?"

"Maybe you were looking to save a little cash?" Carrying an armful of broken wood, Evan traced Ben's steps to the dumpster located just outside the courtyard wall on the north side of the inn.

The sun continued descending toward the horizon line over the ocean. There were probably fifteen more minutes of light.

Ben's gloves were crusted with dirt, so he scrubbed the sweat off his face with a sleeve. "It's possible. When Grandma handed me the reins, the finances weren't in the best shape, and I didn't have a lot in the bank." And still didn't.

They trudged back to the remaining debris, boots

crunching glass and thin, broken tree branches. After chipping away at the rubble all weekend in between other business stuff and family obligations, Ben was thankful he'd nearly cleaned it all up.

"Don't be so hard on yourself, man. I'm pretty sure I could get you some emergency funds. Not a lot. But something." As Walker Beach's assistant community developer, Evan helped hand out grants to struggling businesses.

"Anything would help. But what I really need is guests. People keep canceling because of this damage."

Evan dusted his gloves off onto his pants. "I thought I saw a guest going inside as I pulled up today."

"Yeah, I still can't believe Bella wanted to stay after she saw the wreckage in the courtyard. I mean—" His words cut off as Evan stared at him. "What?"

"Bella?" Evan's brows knit together. "Since when are you on a first-name basis with the guests?"

Ben's cheeks warmed as he strode toward one of the last remaining pieces of jagged wood that had fallen from the porch. "There's only one guest. It isn't hard to remember."

"Probably doesn't hurt that she's good-looking either."

Ben jerked his gaze toward his friend, but Evan just laughed. "It was only a guess, but with that reaction I can see I wasn't far off."

So, she was good looking. That didn't mean anything. Plenty of good-looking women called Walker Beach home.

But Ben hadn't found his thoughts straying to any of *them* during the last three days, which was why, except for brief interactions, he'd avoided Bella since Friday night.

"Whatever. You gonna help me with this?"

"Someone's touchy. Must have struck a nerve." Grinning, Evan helped Ben lift the railing. It strained beneath their arms as they walked it to the dumpster and hefted it inside.

Whew. "Looks like we're mostly done here."

Evan peeled off his gloves and tucked them under his arm. "Let me know when I can help with the actual repairs."

He may get a kick out of busting on Ben, but Evan had turned into a good friend these last few years. "Thanks, bro. You have no idea what that means."

Evan shrugged. "Not like I have much else going on these days. Just working late most nights and looking in on Chrissy."

Chrissy Price, the forty-something-year-old hardware store owner in town, had been a mentor and friend to Evan since he'd stopped his wild ways a few years back. She'd been diagnosed with an aggressive cancer a few months ago and, unfortunately, it looked like she probably wasn't going to make it.

"Well, I appreciate it all the same." Ben would need all the help he could get if he wanted to repair the inn in a few weeks' time. Any longer and he'd miss out on the rest of the high tourism season.

Once again, Ben surveyed the damage along the side of the inn, his gut twisting at the sight. But movement inside the courtyard caught his eye. Someone walked toward them.

Bella.

She'd done away with the professional clothing and wore a yellow tank top and shorts that showed off her shapely legs. Her hair was on the top of her head in a messy knot, and long earrings brushed the top of her shoulders.

Man, she was pretty. And with the casual style, she looked like she belonged here.

Evan nudged him in the ribs. "Looks like *Bella* is coming to say hi."

"Shut up."

They walked forward to meet her inside the courtyard gates. Bella flashed a tentative smile. "Long time, no see." She turned her attention to Evan. "Hi, I'm Bella."

"I know." Evan's eyes sparked with something like amusement. He held out his hand. "Evan Walsh."

She took his offered hand. Evan held on longer than necessary.

Ben had never wanted to punch the guy before, but he wouldn't have minded taking a swing at his friend right now. "He was just leaving."

"Yes, I was." Evan slapped Ben on the back. "Let me know when you need me next, buddy. Bella, a pleasure to meet you." And with that, Evan headed to the parking lot, whistling some obnoxiously upbeat tune.

Ben grunted and turned to Bella. "Did you need something?"

Despite his professional tone, she stiffened. But why? Just because they'd shared a few minutes of pizza and Yahtzee didn't make her more than a guest in his mind, no matter what Evan might say.

"Oh. Yeah. Yes." She cleared her throat. "I just wanted to let you know that my shower isn't working."

He nodded. "I'll get inside and take a look right away."

"No rush. Not until morning, anyway." She offered a wry grin then glanced around the courtyard. "I haven't been back here since your porch nearly killed me. It's tranquil. Well, it will be once you get everything fixed. How long do you think that will take?"

"I don't know. Weeks." She'd be long gone by then.

Not that he cared.

"It would look gorgeous with a garden."

"Maybe. But at this point, I doubt I could even afford the seeds."

"You know seeds are super cheap, right?" Bella leaned against the stone wall ringing the courtyard. "Your finances can't be that bad."

He really shouldn't be talking about this, especially with her, but there was something about the defiance, the certainty, in her voice that made him want to knock her off that high horse. "You wouldn't say that if you got a good look at them."

"So, show me."

Ben huffed out a staccato laugh. "Right." But she was looking at him so openly, as if she hadn't just suggested he show a stranger his vulnerable position. "You're serious." Even after he'd been so rude to her? "What's your angle?"

"Do I need to have one?"

"Doesn't everyone?" He crossed his arms over his chest. "I don't know anything about you. And you don't know me."

"I have an MBA and experience running a business. I can't promise I'll be able to help, but I'm happy to try."

But then he'd owe her.

The wind teased a piece of hair loose from Bella's bun, sweeping it across her face, sticking it to her upper lip. She plucked it free. "Now you know one thing about me. And I already know at least one thing about you. You're a member of town royalty who has the largest family tree in history."

He surprised himself when a chuckle flew from his lips. "In all of history, huh?"

"Fine, maybe not the largest, but definitely bigger than mine. Other than some aunts and cousins who won't talk to me because my mom offended them in some way, my mom is my only family." Bella's eyes fell to the ground. "That I know of."

"That you know of? Are you adopted?" The moment the words left his mouth, he cringed—not only because it was far too personal a question but also because *he didn't care.*

"Not adopted. Just . . . well, not abandoned, exactly." Bella played with one of her earrings then blew out a breath. "I'm here in Walker Beach because I want to find my father's side of the family."

"Are they lost?" His lame excuse for a joke didn't break the tension like he'd hoped.

"They are to me. And I need to know if they're out there."

Something tugged at his heart with those words as she once

again removed her professional veneer. And for just a second, he wanted to offer his help. Anything to chase away her frown.

But that was crazy. Ben barely knew this woman—and he didn't *want* to know this woman. He had his own problems, and he didn't need to add hers to his list.

Except . . . maybe he should. The answer hit him square in the chest.

He considered her for a moment before he spoke. "Bella, what if we helped each other?"

"What do you mean?" She pushed herself off the wall in one fluid motion.

He had her attention. Good. "You help me by looking over my books, seeing if there's any way to turn things around here." Despite all his Walker Beach connections, the only person he could really ask was one who could be objective, who wouldn't be disappointed at the way he'd handled his inheritance. And that meant bringing in an outsider—someone who wouldn't charge him an arm and a leg. "And I'll help you find your father's family."

"How would you do that?" But before he could answer, she shook her head. "Never mind. You don't need to help me. But I'll definitely help you with your accounting."

Oh, she was stubborn but so was he. Ben puffed out his chest. "We help each other or no deal. I refuse to take advantage of your time while you're here." And he would not owe her. Who knew what her price would be?

Man, Elena had really screwed him up, hadn't she?

Bella's eyes narrowed, her gaze like steel. Then, at last, she nodded and held out her hand. "Fine. It's a deal."

Her handshake was as firm and confident as the rest of her. "Tomorrow night? Five-ish?"

"All right then." She walked back toward the inn then stopped and turned. "By the way, I'm going into town to grab some food, so my room will be unoccupied for the next hour if you want to fix the shower now. If not, I'm happy to use a shower in one of the other guest rooms instead."

"Sounds good." If she'd be back in an hour, he'd have her shower fixed in fifty-nine minutes or less.

Ben watched her go, admiring her determination and intelligence—and, yeah, maybe also the way her hips swayed.

Stop it.

Elena had been gorgeous and confident too, but in the end, she'd been his downfall.

Maybe this "deal" was a mistake. But if Ben kept going the same direction with the inn, he'd also keep failing. He needed help.

And it looked like Bella Miranda was his only hope.

Growling, Ben kicked at the dirt and waited until she'd disappeared before he trudged inside too.

CHAPTER 4

*S*py work was not for the faint of heart.

Bella leaned against the brass headboard in her guest room, shutting her eyes and shoving her phone away. But the words from Mom's text message still burned in her mind. *Atta girl. I knew I could count on you to get the job done.*

She fisted soft handfuls of the antique white quilt covering her bed. Mom had sent the text after demanding an update from Bella. It seemed she'd liked that Bella was about to meet with Ben to go over his financials.

If she knew the full truth, though, she'd hate the rest of the facts—that Bella was considering feigning illness and staying locked in her room all evening. Not that she'd need to feign much. She did, in fact, feel sick to her stomach about her upcoming plans with Ben.

And she only had ten minutes to get over it before he expected her down the hallway.

Inhaling deeply, Bella opened her eyes and took in the vertical yellow and white stripes painted on all four walls. Soft light streamed from the corner window beside the bed, and the high wainscot ceiling and crown moldings lent a quiet elegance to the room. Under normal circumstances, it would strike her as peaceful too.

If only she were getting ready to go on a date with a cute guy, not to peek at his financials. If only she were just a girl on vacation, not a company executive sneaking around. If only she could take up Ashley and Shannon on their offer for another lunch without wanting to retch.

Because for one blissful hour on Saturday, she'd almost forgotten she had a job to do. Instead, she'd simply enjoyed time on the beach with two women who were as genuine as they were beautiful. They'd immediately accepted her, almost as if she really belonged in Walker Beach.

Then, reality had crashed in and the illusion shattered.

Because Bella Moody didn't belong anywhere—not even with the only parent she'd ever known. Maybe at one time she had, but not anymore.

Still, maybe another family was out there waiting to accept her with open arms.

She just needed to find them.

Pushing herself off the bed, Bella moved her neck from side to side. She shook her hands and bounced from one foot to the other like she was about to go toe to toe with Rocky Balboa.

She'd need to be on her guard. Rocky hit hard.

Just like any successful boxer, Bella needed a pep talk. "You've got this. Get in, get information, get out. That's your strategy. Stay focused." She couldn't let Ben's piercing gaze distract her. Or the way the blond scruff along his chin winked in the sun against his tan skin. Or how he was so determined to avoid her but had agreed to their little partnership anyway.

Bella cleared her throat. "You've got him right where you want him. Find a way to suggest he should sell. Show him there's no other way to become solvent. Remind him what failure will cost him."

Because Bella couldn't afford to forget what it would cost her.

Her blood pumping a strong beat in her veins, she opened her door then strode down the hallway and the stairs and hooked a left toward the kitchen, which was tucked away on the southernmost part of the building.

Ben sat at the wooden table next to the window that overlooked the beach. Today was slightly overcast, leaving the room on the dimmer side. He looked up from his laptop. "Thanks again for doing this. I really appreciate it."

Bella's heart stuttered. "No problem." As she rounded the table and took the seat beside him, her shoulder brushed his.

His chair legs squeaked against the tile as he backed up. "You want some coffee?" Ben bustled toward the counter where a coffee pot sat. The vintage white cabinets complemented the pale green fridge that looked as if it belonged to the seventies. "I just brewed some. Figured we'd need sustenance."

"Sure, thanks."

He snagged two mugs from one of the cabinets and poured the brown liquid into both. "Cream? Sugar?"

"Both, please."

He brought over the mugs and set them onto the table. "Thought so."

"And why is that?"

"Don't all you big-city types like your frou-frou coffees?" Ben walked back for a small sugar bowl and bottle of hazelnut creamer, which he placed in front of Bella.

"Think you know me so well?" Without adding anything, Bella took a drink from her mug and nearly gagged at the bitter taste.

Ben's eyebrows lifted as he took his seat again. "You sure aren't one to back down from a challenge, are you?" After snagging a spoon from the middle of the table, he measured out a tiny bit of sugar and dumped it along with a teaspoon of cream into his mug. "I guess I should have assumed as much."

"Have you made other assumptions about me?"

"I probably shouldn't say."

"Now you have to tell me." She took the sugar bowl and dumped a good spoonful into her mug. A dollop of cream blended with a nice stir later, and her coffee turned from black to luscious brown. Bella sipped. "Oh, that is so much better."

Chuckling, Ben settled against his chair. "Well, at first I thought you were this big-city executive type used to getting her own way . . ."

"And now?"

He paused. "Wait, that's actually true."

"Hey." She nudged him with her elbow.

"Watch it. You're gonna make me spill."

"It would serve you right." Bella took a drink of her doctored coffee to hide her laugh. Where had this Ben Baker been hiding? She could get used to him.

Get back on track.

Bella set down her mug and pointed at the computer. "Is this ready for me to look at?"

"Yes. But the first thing you need to know is that I've defaulted on my mortgage." He grimaced as his fingers drummed along the edge of his mug.

"You have a mortgage on this? Hasn't it been in your family forever?"

He nodded. "But my grandparents took out a second mortgage to add some rooms onto the south side and build the decking and courtyard, improve the beach, that sort of stuff. And then they had some lean years and didn't pay it off."

"All right." Bella tapped her lips. "How long have you been in default? I'm assuming some fees and extra interest are accruing?"

"Actually, no. I have a buddy who works at the bank, and he's giving me some grace. We don't have anything official in place, but he's agreed to let me push off what I owe and extend the mortgage until I get back on my feet."

Another point for small-town life. "Really? That would never happen in the city."

"People watch each other's backs here." Ben scratched his neck. "Of course, I don't want to take advantage of our friend-ship, so my goal is to pay him back as soon as possible."

He leaned toward the computer screen, peering intently at it. "Anyway, I just wanted you to know that before we get started. So, here's my budget. And here's my spending. And . . ." Ben clicked through his accounting program as he explained the various financials it took to run the inn.

But with his face mere inches from hers, Bella found it diffi-cult to focus. She reached for the laptop. "I'll just take a look for a minute on my own, if you don't mind."

"Go for it." He backed off so she could control the mousepad, but he still wasn't all that far away. His warm breath lifted the hair on her neck, and she closed her eyes, imagining what it might be like to turn her head just slightly, to allow herself to drown in his scent, to wrap her arms around him and find his lips and . . .

"How about some music?" Oops. She'd practically shouted the request, and the curious look on Ben's face evidenced that he might have heard the tremble in her tone.

She snagged her phone and punched in a few commands, selecting the perfect song for the occasion. "Eye of the Tiger" burst from the device.

Ben lifted an eyebrow. "Really like to get pumped up about budgeting, huh?"

"Yep." She turned back to the spreadsheets. "So, where are you at with the insurance?"

"There won't be any." He explained what had happened. "But Evan called this morning and told me I got enough from a small city grant to pay for supplies. It means I can't fully reopen for a while, though, so that's a missed sales opportunity."

Now *that* was information Mom would want to know.

But as the hours ticked by and Bella asked him numerous questions about his financials, as she dug in more deeply, her stomach tightened until it turned into a coil ready to spring.

The truth settled in like a lead weight—Ben wouldn't have much of a shot at surviving the perfect storm he'd found himself in unless he took out a loan or a major infusion of cash came through.

And although Evan was working on getting him a larger grant, it would probably be just enough to pay down the mortgage and maybe a few other annual expenses.

Ben was going under.

Unless Bella helped him.

She could probably do it. This was her area of expertise, after all.

But helping him meant Mom wouldn't help Bella.

Just do it. Tell him there's no way out except to sell.

But the words wouldn't come.

Bella peeked at Ben, took in his pained but hopeful expression, and exhaled a sigh. "I'd like to look at this more in-depth over the next few days. Can you print me a copy?"

"Sure. Absolutely."

Either he finally trusted her, or he was just that desperate. Maybe both.

Was she going to be like Mom and take advantage of that trust?

Bella bit the inside of her cheek, tasting blood. She needed to get out of here, before her resolve weakened any more. "I'll take it to my room and order in."

His lips quirked. "This is Walker Beach. Not many places deliver this far north. Actually, none do during the week."

"Seriously?"

He shrugged. "Welcome to small-town living."

"Yay."

Laughter puffed from Ben's lips. "Come on, let's snag dinner." He placed a hand on top of hers. "My treat."

If Ashley and Shannon could be believed, the fact that Ben was inviting her to dinner—and that she, for once, wasn't the one strong-arming him—was a big deal.

"Are you sure?" Her eyes traveled to their joined hands, which zinged with warmth.

As if just noticing he'd touched her, Ben pulled away his hand, gathered the empty mugs, and headed toward the sink. "We both need to eat, and I don't have much around here." His eyes stayed focused on the water that sprayed from the faucet into the mugs as he scrubbed them hard with a sponge.

"OK."

He fumbled one of the mugs, the ceramic pinging against the side of the sink. His eyes popped up. "Yeah?"

"Sure." Why not? She could gather more intel to feed Mom.

But when he tipped a smile in her direction, her breath caught in her throat, and Bella couldn't help wondering if she'd made a fatal error in judgment.

What had he been thinking, inviting Bella out for dinner?

The second they'd walked into the Walker Beach Bar & Grill, everyone's necks had turned their way—an amazing feat because the huge televisions on the walls blaring the latest sports commentary should have drowned out their entrance.

But Walker Beach residents had a way of sniffing out juicy gossip, and Ben had no doubt that what looked like him being on a date was the juiciest scrap of steak these people would get on a Tuesday night.

Not that it was a date. Nope. They were just two people helping each other out who needed to eat at the same time.

And now that dinner was over, Ben should steer himself back home. Alone. Might be kind of hard to avoid her, though, considering he lived in the same place where Bella was staying, in the room just underneath hers.

Of course, no matter what he *should* do, one fact remained— for the first time since Elena had left him at the altar, he'd spent time with a woman he wasn't related to and hadn't hated it.

"You may need to roll me out of here." Bella patted her stomach and made a face as they swept through the restaurant's front door and into the warm breeze of the summer evening.

The sun was just setting behind the restaurant, which—like most of the restaurants along Main Street—backed up to the boardwalk along Baker Beach.

"You're not the one who downed a double cheeseburger, fries, a Coke, *and* a slice of cake."

Her choice of a six-ounce filet with a side of asparagus and a glass of Malbec had showcased the glaring differences between them—Bella a refined managerial executive from the city, him an uneducated blue-collar worker from Nowhere, USA. Yet still, somehow, they'd found things to chat about over dinner.

The lights along the boardwalk popped on as the sun disappeared. Bella shook her head. "I was sorely tempted to steal a bite of that cake, believe me."

"Why didn't you?" They started down the boardwalk, walking north toward the inn. "You've been pushy before."

"I have not!"

"What do you call trapping me into playing Yahtzee with you last week?" He slipped a smile onto his face and his hands into his pockets.

"*Trapping?* I merely suggested we play. You stayed of your own free will." Bella's responding grin radiated more light than the street lamps above them.

"Uh-huh."

"And though I'll admit I may be pushy about *some* things, isn't it a crime to steal a man's food before the third date?" Her eyes widened. "Not that this was a date. I know we were just . . . eating."

He cleared his throat. "Right."

They were close to the upper edge of town now, with Baker Community Park just beyond. In a hundred feet or so the beach would end, evidenced by the craggy rocks jutting against the ocean and forming the southernmost boundary of the park. The sand here was mostly deserted, though a bonfire glowed down the beach back the way they came. Even the boardwalk wasn't overly crowded, but then again, he'd noticed a lot fewer tourists in town than was usual for this time of year.

Bella nodded toward the beach. "Want to sit for a bit?"

He froze. *Yes. No.*

"Unless you think I'm being pushy by asking." She nudged him with her elbow. "In that case, I definitely don't want to sit on the beach."

He wasn't eager to get back to his spreadsheets, and it was too late to do any repair work on the inn. Ah, what could it hurt? He might as well enjoy the beauty of this summer evening. "If you insist."

"But I don't. That's the point."

"Ha ha."

Smiling, Bella peeled the sandals off her small feet and wove the straps between her fingers, letting the shoes dangle. She stepped onto the sand, and Ben caught up to her but not before her spicy perfume wafted back on the breeze. All night he'd been trying to pinpoint what it smelled like—some sort of cinnamon, he'd decided—because that had been better than focusing on how it was driving him just a little bit crazy.

Bella stopped several feet back from the wet sand and plunked down. Ben joined her, realizing too late how close he'd sat. Even though their shoulders and legs didn't quite touch, the phantom caress of her skin settled over him.

She didn't seem to notice. In fact, Bella was the picture of relaxation, leaning back on her arms, stretching out her feet, and burying her toes in the sand so they just barely peeked through. The full moon above provided enough light for him to glimpse the grains of sand dotting her tan skin.

The ground boomed underneath them, an aftershock that passed quickly.

He pulled his knees into his chest and yanked his eyes toward the undulating waves of the ocean. "You've been here almost a week now. What do you think of Walker Beach so far?"

She took a moment to answer. "It's different from the city, obviously. At first I thought I'd hate the slower pace. It's not in my nature to slow down."

"Kind of guessed that one."

Her laughter added to the cadence of the sea and traveled down his bones. "But there's something really charming about it. I've already met quite a few members of the town."

"And know their life stories, no doubt." Ben rolled his eyes. "Sometimes I could really do without that part of living here."

"I can see how it would be annoying in some respects, but I'm ashamed to say I don't even know my neighbors back home."

He sensed sadness in her tone. "Really?"

"I recognize them, and we say hello as we pass in the hallway, but I don't know their names or anything about them." She sat up straighter. "There's something nice about being anonymous, sure. But sometimes I ache to be known." Her right hand traced a circle in the sand.

"Maybe your neighbors don't know you, but surely you have friends. And a mom."

"My mom and I aren't close." Her hand stilled for a moment

then restarted its comforting, hypnotic pattern. "She is many things but maternal isn't one of them. Not anymore."

"She was once?"

Bella nodded. "A long time ago. I think the combination of night school and working as a maid and waitress when I was in grade school beat it out of her. She became so focused on achieving it all, becoming the CEO of a company, that now she doesn't have time to know who I am."

"That's rough." His arm itched to slip around her shoulders, give her a squeeze. He batted away the impulse. "But believe me, just because everyone in town knows you doesn't mean they *know* you. They only think they do."

"I guess you're right." She eyed him. "But when things go bad, at least you have family to rally around you."

There was something knowing in her gaze. Almost as if . . .

He groaned inwardly. Of course. "Since you've been here longer than a day, I assume you know all about me and my"—he made finger quotes—"tragic and very public heartbreak."

"I may have heard something."

"Probably a whole novel, especially if you've run into Carlotta Jenkins." The forty-something-year-old owner of the self-named clothing boutique had a knack for sniffing out the smallest bit of gossip.

"It was your sister, actually."

"You met Ashley?"

"And your cousin Shannon." Bella brushed bits of sand from her fingertips. "They were sweet—and informative." She shot him a minxy grin.

"I should have known." His chest loosened, and he laughed. "It's too bad you don't have siblings. They make life interesting, that's for sure."

"I wish I did. Maybe . . . maybe I do."

Oh. Right. "If you don't mind me asking, why don't you

know for sure?" He was only asking because he needed to know anyway. To hold up his end of the bargain.

It had nothing to do with how easy she was to talk to. Nope.

"It's not just that I don't know if I have any family." She bit her lip. "It's also that I don't know who my dad was."

Yikes. "Your mom doesn't know?"

"Oh, she does. She just won't tell me anything. Well, not much." Shaking her head, Bella sighed and looked out toward the ocean. "One time I overheard her say his first name was Daniel. But no last name and when I asked about it, she said I needed to leave well-enough alone."

"I notice you use past tense when you talk about him."

"Of the few things she's told me, one is that he died when she was pregnant with me."

"I'm sorry." He tried to infuse enthusiasm into his voice. "But at least you have a starting place. You know he was from here, right?"

"What?" Her head whipped around to look at him.

"I just assumed . . . because you said you were here to find his family."

"To tell you the truth, I'm not sure what I know or don't know." Clouds obscured the moon, creating shadows all around them. "I'm here to figure it all out."

Was she purposefully being vague? No. He was probably reading too much into it. He'd learned to do that after Elena's betrayal. But Bella—there was something different about her. He could feel it. He hadn't known her a week, yet they'd already had a deeper discussion than he remembered having with Elena.

Maybe that had been the problem. One of many, apparently. The other being that Elena had only dated him—the blue-collar handyman—to make her upper-crust parents angry.

"Well, join the club. I'm still figuring out what my life is supposed to look like. The inn, the way I relate to women . . ." He cleared his throat.

A stuttered laugh flew from Bella's lips. "I'm guessing you do just fine with women."

"Being betrayed and lied to by someone who claims to love you tends to do something to a man."

Bella turned her eyes on him again, blinking. She shivered as the wind tousled her hair. "It's getting cold. Guess we should head back."

Yeah. They really should. Because what had possessed him to be so personal with this woman?

What was she doing to him?

She stood and, after a moment, so did he. Without a word, they started toward the boardwalk, the moon peeking through the clouds, watching them as they walked in silence.

CHAPTER 5

*A*ll this time and Bella didn't know if she was any closer to achieving her goal.

Didn't really know if she wanted to be, either.

Taking another sip of her coffee, Bella stared out the floor-to-ceiling back window of the Frosted Cake, which granted her a view of the boardwalk, the beach, and the sparkling water of the Pacific. She'd staked out this corner table early this morning to read Ben's financials in depth once again before their meeting, trying to decide what to do with the information now that she had it.

It wasn't just Ben's hammer pounding and wood planing that had driven her here from the solitude of her room. After their kind-of-not-really date two days ago, her brain—and heart—had been on overload, and she'd needed space to think. Between the high ceilings, circular wooden tables, and eclectic beach-themed decor, the restaurant provided the perfect solution.

Though neither place could drown out her unproductive thoughts about a handsome man on a beach who'd shown her a piece of his heart—probably without meaning to.

"Being betrayed and lied to by someone who claims to love you tends to do something to a man."

Bella squeezed her eyes shut, rubbing them like a thousand particles of dust had gotten stuck inside. Ben's words still haunted her. But not just the words themselves. It was the way he'd spoken them, as if prying open a clam to expose a pearl inside. He'd trusted her enough to tell her what he had.

The problem was that she wasn't worthy of that trust. Which bothered her. A lot.

But still, she had a job to do, a father to find. That was more important than anything else. At least, she'd thought so. So why this tugging inside, this desire to forget what she'd promised her mom so she could deliver what she'd promised Ben?

In looking at his report, it hadn't taken her long to come up with a list of basic things he could change to improve his business practices—raising his prices, for one, and doing some online marketing, for another.

But to share or not to share? That was the question.

Groaning, Bella downed the rest of her coffee and stood to grab some more from the drink station sidebar. In the mornings the Frosted Cake allowed free seating and functioned more like an order-at-the-counter bakery and coffee shop but moved to more traditional restaurant seating and service for lunch and dinner.

As she reached the sidebar, Bella waited behind a woman with poofed-up red hair and long red nails. She poured fresh-squeezed orange juice from a pitcher then turned, looking Bella up and down. Her nose curved at a sharp angle.

"I haven't had the pleasure of meeting you yet." She extended her free hand. "Carlotta Jenkins."

Bella accepted Carlotta's handshake. The woman squeezed harder than necessary. Forcing a smile, Bella squeezed back. "Bella Miranda. I'm a guest at—"

"The Iridescent Inn. I know." A smirk brought out tiny wrinkles around the woman's eyes and lips. "I make it my business to know things about anyone who stays any significant amount of time in my town."

"That sounds exhausting." Finally, someone Bella knew how to handle, unlike everyone else she'd met in Walker Beach. "I'm afraid I don't know anything about you."

Carlotta's smirk wavered before she recovered in a quick moment. A high-pitched jerking laugh tumbled from her mouth. "I own the clothing boutique in the North Village."

The clothing boutique, as if it were the only one. Although, who knew? Maybe it was. Bella shrugged, finally allowing her hand to fall. "I haven't been inside yet." As she poured herself some coffee, the warmth of the liquid seeped through the paper cup into her fingertips.

"Too busy dating our local innkeeper, mmm?" Carlotta's eyes remained hawklike on Bella as she sipped her juice.

Oh, how she longed to take down this woman a notch. Not like she'd be here much longer. She'd either convince Ben to sell or she wouldn't. Regardless of the outcome, Bella wouldn't be sticking around here for the long-term.

But something stayed her tongue. She didn't want to make trouble for Ben—not any more trouble, anyway.

Bella stirred some cream into her coffee with a tiny plastic straw. "Too busy with a lot of things. Excuse me, please." She headed back to her table.

No more distractions. Ben would be here soon. She needed to decide what to do. The papers rustled as she picked them up and studied the numbers, but the figures blurred together.

"Thought you could use this."

Looking up, she found Josephine Radcliffe, the restaurant's owner, holding a plated chocolate long john. "Oh n—"

"On the house."

"Thank you, but I don't need the calories."

"My dear, please consider who you are talking to." The

woman slid a hand up and down her rather voluminous waist-line, which Bella hadn't noticed before. If she'd been asked to describe Josephine, she'd have focused on the proprietor's ready smile. "Now, take my offering before I get offended."

"Yes, ma'am."

"Good." Josephine set the plate on Bella's table and tapped the side of her own nose. "And don't you let the likes of Carlotta Jenkins get to you. I make it a rule never to talk ill about anyone, but if I were to break my rule, she'd probably be the reason."

With a wink, the older woman turned and headed back toward the front counter, which was visible from both sides of the restaurant.

Before Bella could force herself to say no to the chocolate donut, Ben walked into the restaurant accompanied by a balding gentleman whose tan, leathery cheeks spoke of a life-time spent in the sun. When they reached her, Ben pulled out a chair for the other man across the table from Bella and sat between them.

"Bella Miranda, meet Bud Travis. He and his wife own Walker Beach Bar & Grill."

Where she and Ben had eaten on Tuesday night.

They hadn't mentioned their time together since it had happened—unsurprising because she'd spent yesterday confined to her room while catching up on email. Mom had someone covering her workload, but Bella hated the idea of someone else picking up her slack, even if she were here in Walker Beach for the good of the company.

Bella had only known to meet Ben this morning because he'd slipped a note under her door sometime before seven o'clock. She'd assumed they'd be the only two at the meeting and that he was growing impatient to hear about her thoughts on his financials. Thus, the papers spread in front of her.

What was he up to?

She extended her hand. "Pleasure to meet you, Mr. Travis."

The man took her hand, a cheery grin breaking through his bushy white beard and mustache. "Bud, please. And the pleasure is all mine." Just like with Josephine, peace radiated off this man, a sense of belonging that seemed ingrained in him. He knew his place in the world, and Bella couldn't help wishing for the same confidence. Maybe it would come once she knew her full history.

Ben cleared his throat. "Bud has lived here since he was a boy—"

"And I'm old, if you couldn't tell, so that's a long time."

They all laughed.

Ben's fingers fiddled with the edge of one of the report papers. "I figured if anyone would know something about your dad and his family, Bud would."

Oh.

Bella took a drink of her lukewarm coffee, swishing it slowly before swallowing. Why had she ever agreed to Ben's terms? She'd tried insisting she didn't need his help—because the only way he could help was by selling the inn—but he wouldn't budge without her agreement. She'd figured she would be able to get him to fold before he'd remember he was supposed to help locate her family.

She'd figured wrong.

Should have known Ben would be more honorable than that.

"Um, that's great."

Bud cracked his knuckles. "So, young lady, what do you know?"

"Well." She licked her lips. Her eyes wandered the restaurant, landing on a decorative fishing net spread across the wall behind Bud's head. Just like the starfish artfully arranged inside the net, she was caught. Unless she flat-out lied—or could be just vague enough with the details so she didn't.

She'd have to try. Otherwise, she'd be no better than Mom.

Bella returned her attention to Bud. "I only know a few things."

"Ben said as much." He knocked a fist lightly against the side of his head. "But you never know what this old noggin will remember."

Ugh. Here went nothing. "My father's name was Daniel. My mom's name is Camille."

"And you and your mom share a last name?"

"Yes." *Please don't confirm that it's Miranda* . . . She rushed on. "My dad died before I was born."

"And you were born here or somewhere else?" Bud drummed his fingers along the knicked wooden tabletop.

"Los Angeles."

"And they would have been in Walker Beach when?"

She'd never actually said there was a connection between her parents and Walker Beach, but of course Ben would think there was. Why else would she be looking for her father here?

Bella twiddled her earlobe, searching for a way to speak the truth without giving herself away. "Um . . . I was born twenty-seven years ago, and my mom was twenty when she had me."

"And was your mom raised here? Or your dad?"

She stayed focused on Bud, trying to forget Ben was there. It made it easier. Kind of. "I'm not sure where my dad was born, but my mom is from Los Angeles." A droplet of sweat raced down Bella's back.

"Hmmm." Bud sat back in his seat, tugging at the far ends of his beard. "Their names aren't ringing any bells, but a good friend of my wife's may remember more. Being a former teacher, she was involved with the young people back in the day. Maybe she'll know of a couple named Daniel and Camille from twenty-seven years ago. I'll ask her and let you know if she's got anything."

"That . . . that would be great. Thank you."

"Yes, thank you so much, Bud." Ben clapped a hand on the older man's shoulder. "Let me buy you lunch to say thanks."

"Young man, it's my pleasure. You keep that money and spend it on someone a lot prettier than me."

At Bud's comment, Ben snuck a look at Bella and offered her a small smile.

Her heart nearly stopped. Oh boy.

She was in so much trouble.

CHAPTER 6

One major job done. Only five more to go. Plus, about a million smaller ones.

Ben slid off his hardhat and stepped back to examine his handiwork. The northwestern wall of the Iridescent Inn was repaired, minus a new paint job. Dad had done him a solid in sending over his structural engineer to inspect the place earlier in the week, and Ben had breathed a sigh of relief to learn the earthquake damage to the clapboard siding was only superficial and not indicative of a deeper problem.

Groaning, he massaged his sore upper arms, the midmorning Friday sun roasting the back of his neck. Once upon a time, he'd used these muscles on a daily basis, but months behind a desk had clearly weakened him. First, he'd used a backsaw to cut out the damaged clapboard—not an insignificant amount—then he'd cut replacement boards and tapped them into place. Not a terribly difficult process, just a long and tedious one.

And what would have taken a crew of guys one day to complete had taken him three on his own, with help from Evan the last few evenings. Everyone else Ben would have called either had to work or were already busy helping with the other cleanup around town. That's where Dad's company had lent their services, so even if Ben had the money to pay someone to help him out, the crew of Baker Construction was booked for weeks.

As it was, the small grant Evan had managed to secure for him gave him only enough for materials. Still, he'd been grateful for his friend's help.

He craned his neck and caught sight of the damaged bit of the roof on the north side. Just after the quake, he'd thrown some tarp over it to keep out the elements, but that was definitely the next repair. He probably should have taken care of it first, but he'd been waiting for a call back from Dad's roofing guy, who was an expert at repairing older homes. Ben didn't have the funds or time to do a full shingle and underlayment replacement of the entire roof, which was unfortunate because, according to the inn's records, it was long overdue for an upgrade. He could only hope that more damage didn't occur before he had the money to do all of it.

After the minimal roof repair, he'd need to replace damaged boards and railing on the upper porch and—

"Wow, it's looking really great out here."

His eyes swung to the right, stopping on the welcome sight of Bella with a frosty glass of lemonade. "It's coming along. It'll still be another three or four weeks until I can reopen though."

She held out the glass to him. Thanking her, he took it, and she turned to survey his progress, shielding her eyes from the sun overhead.

What was she thinking? Bella hadn't told him any ideas for improving his financials yet, even though she'd been reading the reports at the Frosted Cake when he'd surprised her with Bud Travis yesterday. But he hadn't had a chance to ask after Bud left because she'd scurried away.

Ben didn't want to push, but . . . "I've been meaning to ask if you've had a chance to look over the reports I printed for you. Any more, I mean?" He scraped the ground with his steel-toed boot and downed the lemonade in one fell swoop. The cold rush burned his throat.

She sighed. "I need a few more days. I'm so sorry."

"No, it's all right." It's not like he was paying her for her services, and it's not as if he'd fulfilled his end of the bargain yet. It would likely take time for Bud to get back with them. The city councilman was a busy guy. "I understand."

"Are you at a good breaking point, though? I made lunch."

"You did?"

"OK, fine, I grabbed lunch from the Frosted Cake." She stuck out her tongue. "I do know how to cook, though."

"Prove it."

It took a few seconds, but the smile that had come so easily on Tuesday night reappeared on her beautiful face. "Maybe sometime I will." She took the empty lemonade glass from him. "Now come on."

"Yes, ma'am." Abandoning his hardhat and gloves, he followed her toward the kitchen door. Strange how the damage to the inn had only occurred on the north part of the building and the outer staircase in the middle of the inn, leaving even the upper porch fully intact on the south side.

As they reached the inn, the ground beneath them began to rumble. These aftershocks were getting annoying. Most lasted mere seconds, but every time he had to stop whatever work he was doing and wait them out. During the first several days, hundreds must have occurred.

Bella steadied herself against the doorway. "Whoa, this is a strong one."

The dishes in the sink clanged against the stainless-steel edges, and the inn groaned under the shaking. Something loud cracked somewhere overhead.

"What was that?" Bella asked.

"I'm not sure." Sometimes aftershocks could cause already-damaged buildings to shift just enough that more destruction occurred. *Please don't let that be the case.*

After thirty more seconds, the aftershock ended.

Together they strode outside. His eyes swept the property, stopping on the roof.

On the crack that shot out from under the tarp and now crossed the entire inn.

Ben growled. Great. What was that going to cost him?

More time. More money he didn't have.

"That doesn't look good."

"No." He ran a hand along his jaw, the urge to punch something rushing strongly and fiercely in his veins. "And I'm pretty sure the earthquake insurance I purchased will not cover this since the original damage was from an uncovered event."

"I'm sorry, Ben." Bella placed a hand on his upper arm and squeezed.

The contact surprised him. More surprising was that the friendly gesture didn't have him running for the hills. "No, I'm sorry. You can't stay here anymore. It's not safe."

"I'm not afraid of another aftershock."

"I'm going to have to tackle that roof, and I don't want your room upstairs exposed. I'm sure they have space for you at the Moonstone Lodge. The manager there owes me a favor. I'll call her right now and get you a room."

"I don't want to stay at the Moonstone Lodge." She paused. "Just move me downstairs."

Why was she so determined to stay?

Ben shook his head. "The only other rooms I have are next to mine."

"That works." Bella peeked around him then strode toward an object on the ground. Picking it up, she plopped the yellow hardhat on her head. "Now, put me to work. I don't know much about construction, but I want to help."

He laughed. She looked ridiculous—and fine, adorable—with the oversized hat balancing on her head. And her tone seemed quite serious, which was even more laughable.

Ben waved a hand at her shorts and tank top. "I don't think you're exactly dressed for the occasion."

"I'm sure I have something that will work. Or I can borrow something of yours."

Her comment was said innocently enough, but the thought of her wearing one of his shirts did something to his chest.

"Hey, Ben." They both turned to find Ashley standing just inside the south gate. "And Bella! You're still here. I wondered. What are you guys up to?"

Bella stepped around him and strode toward Ashley. "We were just examining the roof. The latest aftershock damaged it."

Ashley's gaze shot upward. "Yikes."

"Yeah." Ben ran a hand through his hair, and it came back sweaty and dirty.

"Sorry, bro." Ashley came inside the gate. "Listen, I know you're busy, and this probably isn't the best timing, but the whole family is going to Al Fresco Night tonight. I was sent to beg you to come."

"What's Al Fresco Night?" Bella's nose scrunched.

"Every other Friday night during the summer the town hosts a movie in the park night. We set up blankets and chairs, and some vendors sell yummy treats. It's a Walker Beach tradition." Ashley tilted her head. "Bella, you should come with us. You can meet the rest of the Baker clan."

"Oh, I wouldn't want to intrude." But something lit in Bella's eyes at the suggestion. She turned toward Ben. "Are you going to go?"

"I don't know. I'm pretty busy."

"There's always going to be a lot to do, Benjamin." His sister shook her head, smiling.

He *had* been neglecting his family lately, missing more

Sunday night Baker family dinners than he'd made. So, yeah, maybe he was due for a little Baker time.

"All right, I'm in."

And it would be rude not to invite Bella. After all, she was kind of growing on him. He eyed her. "You game?"

And the shy smile she flashed him was proof he'd made the right call. "Let's do it."

Bella got out of Ben's truck and made her way with him from the parking lot into the park. Not Baker Community Park down by the beach but another in the hills that overlooked the downtown area. Up this way, the landscape turned residential, the mature California oak trees providing a gorgeous contrast to the beach setting below.

The movie would begin in fifteen minutes, and the parking lot was packed as they weaved their way toward the enormous grassy field. A paved walking path surrounded the park, and baseball fields held space in the far corner. The huge projector screen stood tall in the grass, close to the playground equipment where dozens of children took advantage of the last vestiges of daylight. About a dozen food trucks lined the edge of the parking lot, producing a variety of sweet and salty smells that left Bella's stomach growling.

"My family usually sits that way." Ben nodded toward the screen as he adjusted the straps of two collapsible camping chairs flung over his shoulder. Freshly showered, he smelled of clean shampoo and wore jeans and a black Walker Beach High hoodie with its sleeves pushed up to his elbows.

"Great."

When he turned her way, something about how he looked at her caught her breath. It was more than just his handsome features and muscles, which were distracting to say the least.

But it was the tinge of vulnerability lacing his expression that Bella longed to touch. Exhaustion she longed to ease. And, somehow, she wanted nothing more than to help him keep his family heritage intact. To help him keep his inn.

She closed her eyes as the weight pressing against her chest deepened. Because that was the opposite of what she was supposed to do.

Ben bumped her shoulder. "You look queasy. Sure you want to hang out with my crazy family all night?"

No. What if they saw right through her? But the allure of a big family event was too much to pass up. And if she happened to get to sit next to Ben in the dark . . . well, that was just a bonus. "Of course."

"Only about ten more seconds before you can back out." He glanced back at the park, squinting. "Scratch that. We've been spotted."

Bella's leg muscles twitched. Too late to turn and run all the way back to the inn, then. Definitely too late to run back to LA.

Normally, she could push through any feelings of nervousness. She laughed in the face of a big board meeting where she was presenting a new idea. Stood strong when forced to fire an employee. Braced herself before facing Mom in any capacity.

But meeting Ben's family? It was different. And it wasn't just about work. Not anymore.

As they approached the grassy area, which was already a flood of picnic blankets and lawn chairs, a tall woman with a ponytail turned from her conversation with two others. Her face lit up. "Ben! You made it." Striding toward him, she pulled him in for a hug.

"Hey, Mom." He pulled back from the embrace and turned. "This is Bella. She's staying at the inn."

Bella forced a swallow as the woman's kind eyes shifted toward her. "Hi, Mrs. Baker." She held out a hand. "Nice to meet you."

"Lisa, please." The woman stepped forward and, before Bella knew it, had her arms around Bella's shoulders. She smelled like jasmine and lemon, and her embrace wasn't casual—it was a real mom hug, deep and tender and welcoming, the kind Bella hadn't experienced in a long time.

When Ben's mom lowered her arms, her smile gave off the same warmth as a hot cup of cocoa. "Such a pleasure to meet you. Ashley mentioned you may be here."

"I hope I'm not intruding."

"Oh, nonsense." Her arm looped through Bella's. "Come on. I'll introduce you to the family." She started to walk, forcing Bella to keep up. "Kiki, Louise, this is Bella, a friend of Ben's."

Both women, stylish fifty-somethings with highlighted blond hair and thin waistlines, greeted Bella just as warmly as Ben's mother had. Lisa patted Bella's hand. "These are my sisters-in-law. Well, two of them anyway."

They all laughed as if she'd said some hilarious joke. But it wasn't the typical fake laugh of The Plastics in the corporate world Bella had known for the last ten years—ever since Mom's business venture had catapulted them from poverty to riches almost overnight. No, this was all sweaters and fireplaces and cozy summer evenings curled up reading a good book.

Before Bella could say anything else, a few more family members joined them, and Lisa made another round of introductions.

Bella recognized one of the women from her first day in Walker Beach. "Jules, your art gallery is amazing."

Ben's redheaded aunt didn't look a day over thirty-five in her sleeveless white boho dress and long feather necklace. "That's so sweet. And what do you do, Bella?"

Everyone's attention swiveled to Bella. She gulped, angling her head backward to find Ben smirking about ten feet away. Clearly, he was enjoying seeing her swallowed by the Baker tide. Returning her attention to Jules and the others, Bella smiled, praying it didn't look as thin lipped as it felt. "I'm a manager at a company in Los Angeles."

"What kind of company do you work for?"

At the question, which was innocent enough, a small fire started in the pit of Bella's stomach. "Well . . ."

"Bella! You're here." Ashley whizzed from somewhere outside the circle of aunts, which parted. Ben's sister snagged Bella's hand and tugged. "I have a spot saved for you and Ben up front."

Before anyone could protest, the two made their way closer to the movie screen. "I thought you could use a rescue, and Ben was too engrossed in playing with our littlest cousins to notice."

Scanning the area, Bella finally located Ben on the ground, dog piled underneath three small children, laughing. The sight did something to her insides.

Capable handyman. Family guy. Child wrangler.

What was Bella doing here? If she had any heart at all, she'd leave this amazing man and his family alone. Coming here had been a grave error. Yet she couldn't gather the strength to go.

"I didn't need rescuing." Bella tucked a wayward strand of hair behind her ear. "Your family is nice."

"But overwhelming. And, sorry, I'm about to introduce you to more." Ashley stopped at a cacophony of blankets placed side by side and occupied by a few dozen younger adults who were talking and laughing together.

"Hey, guys." Cupping her hands around her mouth, Ashley raised her voice. "Listen up. This is Bella, a friend of mine who's visiting from out of town."

The whole gang stopped what they were doing and shouted a round of hellos.

"Nice to meet you, everyone."

By this time, the sun had fully disappeared, floodlights illuminating the edges of the park. A suave older man tapped on a microphone set off to the side of the big screen. "If everyone would find their seats, the movie is about to start."

"You and Ben, wherever he is, can sit here." Ashley plopped next to Shannon, who was busy talking to someone else, and Bella sat beside Ashley, leaving just enough space for Ben between her and a blond woman. She was holding hands with a muscular guy similar looking to Ben.

The woman glanced her way. "Ah, another outsider."

"Excuse me?"

"You had a bit of a wide-eyed look about you. I get it. We're surrounded by Bakers. It takes a little getting used to their number." The blonde smiled back at the man, who was engaged in another conversation. "I'm Gabrielle Wakefield." A one-carat white-gold ring on her fourth finger winked in the lamplight.

"Ah. I'm Bella. So, you're marrying into the family?"

Her fiancé swung his head their way. "In two long months." He kissed Gabrielle's cheek then stuck out his hand toward Bella. "Tyler Baker. Ashley's cousin."

She shook it. "Nice to meet you both."

"You're here with Ashley?"

"Um, kind of."

Just then Ben lowered himself to the ground. "Hey, sorry to leave you to the wolves." He turned toward Tyler, who was looking between Bella and Ben, grinning. "What's up, man? Hey, Gabrielle."

Microphone feedback squawked through the speakers as the man up front adjusted it. "Welcome to Al Fresco Night. For those who don't know me, I'm Mayor Jim Walsh, and I'd like to thank you for your patronage. Remember, 10 percent of all food purchases go toward our earthquake relief fund. We're all in this together."

Beside her, Ben huffed.

She leaned in. "Not a fan?"

"That's Evan's dad. He's . . . well, let's just say that those of us who know him well enough always take what he says with a grain of salt."

The mayor droned on about the importance of continuing to act like a real community, pulling together in times of trial.

"How did he get elected then?" Bella angled her face next to Ben's ear so he could hear her. Her skin buzzed at their proximity.

"Guess he fooled enough people." He shrugged. "But from what Evan has told me, he's willing to cut corners when necessary as long as it gets him what he wants."

Just like her mom.

Mom, who would surely pull Bella from the field if she knew how her heart was deviating from the mission.

Bella fidgeted with the sleeve of her cardigan, which she was grateful to have worn, considering the chill that had just come over her.

"Are you cold?"

And before she could answer, he was unzipping his sweatshirt.

"Stop. You'll be cold then."

The movie's opening credits rolled, and the din of the crowd fell away.

"I'll be fine." He looped the hoodie around her shoulders, and the smell of him surrounded her. Not just the clean shampoo but a tiny hint of coffee and some sort of spicy cologne he must wear sometimes.

Her toes curled.

"Thanks." Bella looked up into Ben's eyes. An intensity burned there—something hidden behind his gaze.

He started to pull his arm away, but Bella reached up to grab his hand. Their gazes still connected, he flexed his hand inside hers for a moment. Her heart hammered in her throat.

Abort. Abort!

But then Ben tightened his hold, drawing her closer until her head rested against him. Not saying a word, he twined their fingers together.

And she couldn't help the sigh that escaped as her whole body relished being cocooned and safe in someone's arms. But not just anyone's arms. The arms of the man who had, somehow, begun to change her perspective.

Being out among this community, feeling the goodwill and the kindness in the air, Bella knew Ben was right. This town didn't need a huge resort like the one Mom wanted to build. The flood of tourists and traffic, the inevitable chain restaurants and shops that would follow—they would take the charm of the place and destroy it. Change it, at the very least.

And not one thing about this place needed to change.

Something settled in her empty gut. Something hard and pointy but solid and . . . right. Bella knew what she had to do.

CHAPTER 7

*H*ad last night really happened?

Ben pocketed his keys as he left the parking lot that divided the South Village from the North Village on Main Street. The sky was clear of clouds, the sun beat down a jaunty tune, and the rich memory of last night's movie in the park drifted on the breeze.

Not just the way he'd held Bella close, stroking his thumb across the top of her hand, reveling in the feel of her, the smell of her flower-scented hair, the bond over shared moments of laughter during the comedy playing out on the big screen.

But also the way his chest had tightened when he'd seen her hugging his mom, talking with his sister, getting introduced to his million and one cousins—and handling it all like a boss, with no hint of intimidation or the desire to flee.

It was so different from Elena, who had constantly tried dragging him away from his family. Who'd wanted to move away from Walker Beach after having been "trapped" there for most of her life.

OK, so maybe his judgment had been off when he'd selected Elena as a wife. But given what he'd seen last night—what he'd seen since he met Bella, really—he could sense that maybe, just maybe, she was different.

Dense as it sounded, he hadn't even known until last night that he'd started to develop real feelings for her. Not just a slight flirtation or physical attraction, but . . . well, he didn't know what.

While passing a billboard on his way toward the hardware store, a bright purple flier for the Olallieberry Festival happening a week from today caught his attention. He'd nearly forgotten about the annual town event—unsurprising given all the havoc wreaked by the earthquake. All of Walker Beach plus a ton of tourists from surrounding cities attended the festival, which featured craft, jewelry, and art vendors as well as live music and tons of delicious olallieberry treats.

Could make a nice first date.

The thought popped into his mind so suddenly that Ben stumbled. As he picked up walking again, the idea stewed and simmered.

Sure, they'd had a nice time last night, but she didn't live in Walker Beach. In fact, she was as big city as they came. Used to the finer things in life. And there was still so much he didn't know about her.

But maybe asking her out was the way to find out if this . . . something . . . could ever lead anywhere.

He'd have to think on it some more. But . . . maybe.

At the southern tip of Main Street, just before the beachfront golf course took over the landscape, Hole-in-the-Wall Hardware came into view. A bell jangled as he entered the store and waved at Chrissy Price.

"How's my favorite innkeeper?" The forty-something shop owner smiled, but something wasn't quite right about it. Or maybe it was the sunken cheeks, the bags beneath her eyes, the way she slumped on her stool behind the big oak register, that were wrong. The headscarf covering her bald head featured lemons and pitchers of lemonade. Its bright blues and yellows matched the rest of the store.

Ben maneuvered past a few other residents browsing the shelves. "I'm all right. And how's my favorite babysitter?" Chrissy was only fifteen or so years older than Ben and, like him, had lived in Walker Beach her entire life. She was a staple in the town, and the thought she might not be here much longer was a shot in the heart of the entire community.

Chrissy's jolly laugh dissolved into a cough.

Before Ben could find her some water, Aunt Jules strode from the back with a water bottle. "I thought I was your favorite babysitter. And here." She shoved the bottle into Chrissy's hand. "I still think you should be at home resting." She and Chrissy had been best friends for as long as Ben could remember.

"I'll rest when I'm dead, Jules." Chrissy's eyes twinkled despite her morbid joke.

"Don't say that." Jules's voice wavered.

Ben had always thought of his aunt as the strongest of her siblings, the most determined, the most independent, but it was easy to see that strength falling away in the face of a situation she didn't have any control over.

Ben cleared his throat. "Well, hey, I need to snag a new air compressor so I can start fixing my roof. I know you have great people in your corner already, but let me know if there's anything I can do for you, Chrissy."

"Thank you, Ben. I'm blessed, that's for sure." Chrissy's eyes crinkled. "I heard the damage was pretty bad up your way. I hope it's nothing serious." She took a swig from her water.

"Nothing Ben can't fix, right?" Aunt Jules winked at him and folded her arms over her chest. "Although from what I saw last night, there may be a little distraction that could delay his progress."

Great. The Walker Beach rumor mill probably already had

him and Bella married less than twenty-four hours after she'd attended an event with him.

"Ooo. Do tell." Chrissy leaned forward.

He shook his head. "Nothing to tell."

But Aunt Jules waved aside Ben's protest. "A woman, his date last night. Met her and liked what I saw so far. And I really liked seeing Ben so happy."

"Aw, that's so wonderful. Ben, you deserve to be happy."

"Aunt Jules is exaggerating. Bella was not my date. Ashley invited her."

"Don't you call me a liar, Ben Baker. I know what I saw." Aunt Jules turned knowing eyes toward Chrissy. "Definitely a distraction waiting to happen."

"I really hope that's not what she is."

Ben winced at the booming voice coming from behind him. He turned to find a broad-shouldered man holding a new red toolbox. "Hey, Dad."

"Son, what are you doing here?" Despite his fifty-five years, Frank Baker was nearly as fit as Ben, and, miraculously, he still had a full head of brown hair streaked with gray. He set the toolbox on the counter in front of Chrissy and Aunt Jules, whom he acknowledged with a nod. "Figured you'd be using every daylight hour possible to fix up your place. I don't imagine you're getting much business in its current shape. Must be hard on the pocketbook."

Though Ben had texted with Dad a few times during the last two weeks about the condition of the inn, he'd avoided any conversation about his financial situation. And until now, Dad hadn't asked.

"I'm just here to grab an air compressor." Ben scrubbed the back of his neck with his hand. "Mine is busted."

"Could have borrowed mine."

"I need a working one anyway. And you're already letting me

borrow some of the other tools I need." He waved to Aunt Jules and Chrissy. "I'll be back in a bit. See you later, Dad."

Before his dad could ask any more questions, he headed toward the corner where Chrissy kept the air compressors. Ben studied the various options, weighing the pros and cons of a more budget-friendly choice with a more powerful one suited to the task he needed to complete.

"You really should buy a more professional-grade machine, you know."

Ben briefly closed his eyes before flicking his attention toward his dad's hulking form. "Probably."

"So why aren't you?" Dad's eyes reflected the same hard flint as when Ben was a teenager who'd snuck out for the first—and last—time. Ashley called them his truth-ferreting eyes.

If Dad were on the hunt, then there was no use in trying to hide stuff from the old bulldog.

Sighing, Ben leaned against the dusty shelf. "I may be in some trouble. Monetarily speaking."

"Define trouble."

Oh man. This was going to hurt. Any respect his dad had for him was about to slide away like drops of water down a shower drain. Ben's gaze fell onto the wooden floorboards. "Take your pick of definitions, but I'm in the hole. I didn't have earthquake insurance, apparently. And while I didn't have a lot to begin with, most of my July and early August reservations have canceled." Ben shook his head. "If I don't figure something out, I'm going to lose the inn."

"You're not thinking of selling, are you?"

Ben's head shot up. "No."

"Good. Because that property has been in our family for more than a hundred years. Your great-great-grandfather built it from nothing."

As if he hadn't heard that before. But as the oldest of five siblings, Dad took his position as head of the Baker clan seriously and felt the occasional need to remind everyone of their familial duties.

"I know, Dad." He puffed out his chest a bit. "Don't worry about it. I didn't tell you because I want your help. I'm going to figure something out without selling and without losing it to the bank. Bella is helping me look over—"

"Maybe that's the problem."

"What do you mean?"

"Seems to me your priorities aren't where they should be." Dad clapped a hand on Ben's shoulder. "Son, I know that Elena did a number on you. It's a good thing I don't know where she lives because I have half a mind to find her and give her a stern talking to."

Ben huffed out a caustic laugh.

Dad's squeeze dug into Ben's collarbone. "And then I'd punch the daylights out of that man she left town with."

"If she's even still with him." Because Elena traded in men on a whim—after an afternoon spent reveling in their company, in laughing over their corporate exploits, in dreaming of a different kind of life, one that didn't include an uneducated small-town guy like Ben Baker. "But Dad, my problems started long before Bella got here. She's got nothing to do with any of this. She's just helping me figure out how to dig myself out of the pit."

He hoped she could, anyway. Maybe he'd ask her again. But he didn't want her to feel used, especially now that there might be something more between them.

"I hate to contradict you, son, and believe me, I don't want to hurt you when I say this, but you allowed Elena to distract you. To take your eye off the prize. And maybe, just maybe, you're doing it again."

"That's not what's happening." At least, he didn't think so. "She's helping me."

"I know you like her, and I know she's beautiful, and I know she charmed the pants off the whole family, but—"

"There's more to her than that."

"What do you really know about her, Ben?"

Dad had him there. The woman had given him bits and pieces, but her past—even her current life—were shrouded. But those things didn't comprise a person, anyway. He knew who she was.

Didn't he?

Shoving aside his doubts, he looked Dad in the eye. "I know enough." For now.

Dad rubbed the bridge of his nose. "I'm just looking out for you. From what I can tell, she's a nice girl. But she's also a big-city type, and those folks tend to go back to what they know. They have different priorities than us."

"It's not like I'm proposing marriage to her tomorrow."

"Just don't go losing your heart to her. Focus on what's most important right now—saving your inn—and if she's still around when that's done, then maybe you can see where things go." Snagging the most expensive air compressor off the shelf, Dad loaded it onto a dolly sitting next to the display.

"I can't afford that one, Dad."

"I've got it." His dad started toward the front of the store, compressor in tow.

"No, I—"

"Hush up, son." Dad swung around. "I may not be able to dig you out of the hole, but I can hand you a shovel. Remember the people who really care about you and you'll be all right."

"I expected you home by now."

Bella kicked the pile of sand underneath her feet. Mom's voice in her ear grated against the solitude of the setting.

She'd come down to the Iridescent Inn's private beach to think about how best to approach the conversation with her mother. But now that she was having it, logic was leaving her brain.

Only the high of the emotions left over from last night—from when she'd felt part of a family, a town—remained.

And the cold reality that she was just an interloper, a pretender. That she'd be going back to her real life soon enough. That no matter what she did, she couldn't change that she was the daughter of the woman trying to steal a piece of Ben's history out from under him.

When Bella didn't answer, Mom doubled down. "I also expected more updates along the way." The familiar sound of Mom's swiveling chair squeaked across the line. Of course she was at work on a Saturday afternoon. Why wouldn't she be?

Bella stared down the empty beach, where the water crashed against the lonely shore. "There have been some . . . developments."

"What developments? The last I heard from you, you'd gotten ahold of his financials but refused to send them over until you'd looked at them." She paused. "Well? Is he going to fold? Or does this earthquake actually give him a leg up thanks to insurance?"

Bella wiggled her toes into the sand, soaking in the warmth given by the midday sun. "He didn't have earthquake insurance."

Mom laughed, clear triumph in it. "That's certainly a development. What else have you learned?"

Why couldn't Bella just let herself lie? It would be so much easier. But after watching her mom do it day in and day out—*"I promise I'll be there, baby"*—Bella had sworn she'd only ever say what she meant. Omitting the truth was as close as she'd come and even that was starting to feel like more of the same.

A sigh left her lips. "He's broke, OK? On the verge of financial collapse."

"Now, was that so hard to tell me? This is great news. What are your next steps to push him toward selling?"

And here it went—the plea to her mother's humanity, if she had any left. "To tell you the truth, I'm not sure I should anymore."

"Come again?" Disapproval seethed from Mom's tone.

"You heard me, Mom."

"And I can't believe what I'm hearing. Don't you know what's at stake here, Bella?"

Bella walked to the edge of the water, and when a wave crept over her toes, its cold temperature shocked her after the warmth of the dry sand. But after a few moments its effects on her skin diminished. "If you'd just tell me what I want to know about my father, then—"

"Your fath—" Mom exhaled with such force that static crackled over the line. "The stakes are much higher than that. You're thinking small potatoes, a flash in the pan. Bella, if we don't get that inn, then the other properties we purchased—at premiums, mind you—are going to tank us. We need to secure that property—and soon—or this project could drive us into bankruptcy."

"Bankruptcy?" A breeze whistled across the beach, taking her hair hostage for a moment before settling down. "How?"

"The resort will be a huge profit-driver for us, but we need to complete it before we can actually gain said profits. You know that."

"Obviously. But why will it bankrupt us? Last time I looked, I thought we were sitting fine."

"A few of our other prospective projects have fallen through." Mom's voice steeled. "In short, you can't fail me."

So Bella was supposed to be there for Mom even though her mother had not been there for Bella in so many ways? "Why not sell the properties on either side of Ben's and start over in another community more willing to play ball?"

"No. It has to be Walker Beach."

Squinting as she looked up and down the beach, Bella understood the appeal. Still . . . "Mom, there are other beautiful properties, other small towns, along the coast."

"Drop it, Bella."

Was that an edge of anger? Why? Her mom had been calmer that time she'd gone toe to toe with attorneys threatening to sue the company over a supposed breach of contract.

Finally. A crack in Mom's armor. Maybe she had a heart underneath all that iron after all. "I can't. I deserve to know."

"Walker Beach is where I met your father, all right?"

Whoa. That's definitely not what Bella had expected to hear. Her heart clobbered her sternum. "What?"

"I was young and I . . ." Mom halted. "I'll tell you the rest of the story once you've secured Ben Baker's signature on the dotted line."

And there was the mother she knew. Bella wasn't going to get anything more from her. For now. "I'll let you know when I have something to share." Then she hung up and plunged the phone into the back pocket of her jean shorts.

Despite her attempts, her mom wasn't going to budge. Bella's noble efforts to find her way out of her predicament—to choose her family or to choose Ben and his—had been for naught.

But no, she'd learned something. A tiny inkling of a something but more than she'd known before this moment. All this time what she'd allowed Ben and Bud Travis to believe might actually be true.

Her father might be from Walker Beach.

What if she could find out about him without Mom's information? Then she wouldn't have to betray Ben. It might even mean she could explore the feelings firing between them. If he knew she'd chosen a relationship with him, maybe he'd forgive her for her initial deception when she told him the truth.

"Slow down, Bella." She was getting ahead of herself. There was still the possibility that Bud was going to come up empty and that the little information she had would lead her nowhere, leaving her to rely on Mom once again.

But what if?

She allowed the thought to linger as she trudged back up the path from the beach toward the inn. Ben hadn't been around when she'd come out of her room this morning, but she spied his truck in the parking lot now. This was as good a time as any to ask him if he'd heard back from Bud with any leads.

Bella quickened her pace then entered the inn and wandered the hall toward his office. She didn't see him inside, so she made her way to the front desk. Not there either. She tried the kitchen and found him unboxing some sort of heavy-duty tool.

"Hey."

He turned at her greeting. "Oh. Hey." His eyes flitted back to the unboxing as he flung an egg crate and plastic wrapping onto the tabletop.

Huh. Definitely not the greeting she'd anticipated after last night. "Something wrong?"

Shaking his head, he pulled a black and yellow metal air compressor from the box. His muscles strained with the movement.

Maybe he was just busy. She'd come back with her question later. "OK. I'll leave you to this, then."

"Wait." Ben faced her. His forehead wrinkled. "Sorry. I just saw my dad, and now I'm thinking about everything. Like how I'm going to financially swing saving the inn. So, I guess I just need to know. Can I? Or is it a lost cause?"

And here another golden opportunity had presented itself— to tell him his only option was to sell and get what she wanted.

But maybe what she wanted was changing.

Bella bit the inside of her cheek and decided. "Don't give up just yet. I have a few ideas we can try." She hadn't yet fleshed out a full plan, but a handful of obvious ideas that wouldn't take much time to formulate into an actionable business plan existed.

Ben's shoulders lifted as he strode toward her. "Really?" A smile lit his face.

"Really."

A laugh tumbled from his lips, loose and triumphant. "Thank you." Then he wrapped her tightly in a hug. She swallowed hard as she listened to his heart beating in time with her own.

He pulled back and released her far too soon. "You have no idea what this means to me. I only wish I could do something equally as great for you."

"Have . . . have you heard back from Bud yet?" A tremor overtook her chin, and she choked back the emotion in her voice. What if nothing ever came of the hopes that had barreled through her only five minutes ago?

"Aw man, I can't believe I forgot. Bud pulled me aside as I was leaving the hardware store, but I was distracted." He slipped his hand into his pocket then pulled out a torn piece of notebook paper. "Well, anyway, he gave me this."

She snatched the paper from his outstretched hand and studied it. "It's an address and phone number. Who's Mary Robinson?"

"The former teacher Bud mentioned. I guess she wants to talk with us about a possible lead on your dad. She can meet on Monday afternoon."

"Really?" Bella gripped the paper in her fingers, trying to identify the feeling welling up in her chest.

Hope.

For only the second time—the first being when Mom agreed to their arrangement—she held hope in her hands.

But . . . "What if it doesn't lead to anything?" The paper fluttered onto the floor.

He picked it up, pressed it back into her hands. "Then we keep searching."

We. She liked the sound of *we.*

Bella cleared her throat past the welling emotion. "Will you come with me?"

"Of course I will."

For a moment, they stood there, eyes locked. Her mouth went dry. What would it be like to be worthy of that look of trust, of awe, of perhaps something even deeper in his eyes? To lean into him, into whatever was happening between them?

To kiss him?

Her fingers reached out to snag his T-shirt, tugging him closer. He came willingly and slid an arm around her waist. With the pad of his thumb he caressed her upper lip, tracing it from top to bottom.

Her breathing shallowed, but she didn't pull away.

Ben dipped his head, his mouth hovering over hers.

"Yo, Ben! You in the—oh."

Bella jerked her head at the intrusion and Ben stepped back, letting go of her waist.

Evan leaned against the kitchen doorway, a grin plastered to his face. "Sorry to interrupt. Just came to help with the roof. We *did* have plans, didn't we?" His eyebrows waggled. "Because if plans have changed, I can go."

Yes, plans had most definitely changed. Bella gripped her forehead. "No, I'll go."

Ben glanced at her beneath his furrowed brow.

Before he could say anything, she forced a smile. "I have a business plan to draw up, after all. Hope you get a lot done on the roof today." Then she turned on her heel and strode back to her room, lips still tingling as she walked.

CHAPTER 8

*M*ary's house was four miles north of town, on a stretch of dirt road that led toward a handful of vineyards. Ben hadn't been there before, but he was familiar with the area because his buddy Derek's family lived out this way. His truck kicked up dust as they passed rolling green foothills, shrubs, and juniper trees. Wispy clouds decorated the brilliant blue of the sky.

He glanced over at Bella in the passenger seat. As she stared out her window, her right hand gripped her left upper arm, alternately squeezing and letting off the pressure. She'd been quiet almost the entire way here, leaving the silence to be filled by the country music artists serenading them from Ben's stereo.

"It'll be OK." Keeping one hand firmly on the wheel and his eyes on the road, he reached out his right hand.

A few seconds later, she gripped it. "I hope so."

He did too, especially because she'd been kind enough last night to sit down with him and discuss her thoughts about how he could get the inn back on track. In many ways, her ideas were simple. And yet, he hadn't been doing them. They'd stayed up way too late outlining the best ways to implement her strategy, and later he'd dragged himself into bed and slept hard for the first time in months.

As they pulled into the driveway of Mary's house, Ben shut off the ignition and squeezed Bella's fingers. "Let's find out the truth about your family."

Her jaw clenched, but she nodded and pulled herself upright. A calm, cool professionalism transformed her expression, putting it in neutral. This must be how she looked at work before a big meeting. "All right. Let's go."

They climbed from the vehicle and walked toward the blue bungalow. While the small, tidy flower garden in front was full of purple and yellow blooms, the peeling paint covered most of the siding, and a crack in the loft dormer window highlighted the building's age. A rusty red tricycle lay on its side next to the garden. As they walked toward the veranda steps, Ben also spotted some damage to the sloped roof.

As far as he knew, Mary Robinson didn't have any family except her thirty-something daughter who had recently run off, leaving her young son in Mary's care. If she'd let him, Ben would gather some guys to help fix up the old place when he was done repairing the inn.

Once they'd mounted the steps, Bella rang the doorbell and exhaled a steady stream of air. "I know you had to give up work time to be here, so thank you."

"No worries. I made some good progress on the roof this weekend. Besides, this is where I want to be." Not for the first time since they'd nearly kissed in the kitchen on Saturday, he contemplated leaning down and trying again. But something held him back. Besides, this moment was all about *her*, not them. He was just along for support.

The door squeaked open, and a pair of pale blue eyes stared back at them. "Hello." A petite woman with curly gray hair peeked out. "Can I help you?"

"I'm Ben Baker, ma'am, and this is Bella Miranda."

No recognition flickered on her face. She scrunched her nose. "Who?"

A flash of red zoomed through the door and between Bella and Ben, forcing them to drop their hands.

"Noah Robinson!" Mary opened the door wider. "You get back here this instant."

Ben turned to find a young boy with a mop of blond curls running around the grassy front yard in a red cape.

"I'm Superman! I'm Superman!" Noah, who looked to be three or four, extended one arm in front of his body and emitted airplane noises as if he were flying.

Mary marched onto the porch. "Superman, come back here now, please." Though her tone was pleasant enough, there was something weary in it.

When Noah ignored Mary's command, Ben tilted his head. "Allow me, Mrs. Robinson."

"Bless you." She sank onto a porch chair.

Ben hauled himself down the steps. "Hey, Superman, want to fly for real?"

The boy halted in his tracks. "Yes!" He pumped his little fist in the air.

With a backward glance at Bella, who had taken the seat next to Mary, Ben scooped up Noah and ran all over the yard with him in both arms. Together they whooped and hollered before Ben delivered Noah to the porch. He knelt in front of the little man. "Now, I need you to execute an important mission. Do you think you can do that?"

With wide eyes, Noah nodded. Even with peanut butter smeared around his lips, the kid exuded cuteness.

"I need you to go to your room, grab your favorite book, and look at the pictures until your grandma tells you otherwise."

"That's not a mission." Frowning, Noah slid a finger toward his nostril.

Ben caught the offending finger and lowered it—and his

voice—as he leaned in. "Believe me. It is. And I'm counting on you."

"Really? OK!" Noah flew up the steps and into the house, banging the front door behind him.

Trudging up the steps, Ben leaned against the porch railing and faced the two women. "What did I miss?"

Bella smiled, but there was something shaky in it. "I reminded Mary why we're here."

The older woman waved a hand in the air. "I remembered. It just . . . took me a minute." She leaned back in her chair, crossing her arms. "Thank you for your help with Noah. He's a wonderful boy, just a bit high-spirited."

"You're his guardian now?"

Mary frowned at Ben's question then nodded. "Julie should be back in a month or two. This isn't the first time she's run off to 'find herself.'" She poofed up the roots of her hair and faced Bella again. "Now, then, back to you, my dear. You said your father was Daniel, but you don't know his last name. And your mother Camille? What was her last name?"

Bella's mouth flopped open then closed again. What had her so tongue tied? Maybe this was all overwhelming despite her attempt at a brave front.

"Miranda," Ben volunteered.

Her brow furrowed, Mary pinched her bottom lip with twitching fingers. "I told Bud I remembered them, but that Camille had a different last name. Can't think of it off the top of my head but maybe it'll come to me later."

Bella sat forward. "Do you remember Daniel's last name?"

Mary scratched her jaw. "I just can't seem to recall."

"Do you remember anything about him? Was he from Walker Beach? Does he have any family left? What did he look like?"

"I . . ." Squeezing her eyes, Mary's mouth trembled. The woman was clearly exhausted. A young boy was a lot of work for anyone, much less a seventy-year-old who lived alone outside town. "I'm sorry."

Ben pushed away from the railing. "Maybe we should come back another day."

Bella's gaze shot to him, her lips in a frown. But after a moment of silent challenge, her shoulders sank. "I guess so. Mary, we didn't mean to upset you."

The woman's eyes flickered open. "You didn't upset me, my dear. I upset myself. Things are sometimes crystal clear. Other times . . . Well, it's hard getting old." She pushed out a forced laugh. "I will think about it some more and write anything down that comes to me. How's that?"

"Sure. Of course." Bella touched her arm. "Is there anything we can help you with while we're here?"

"Your young man helped plenty simply by getting my grandson into the house. Noah loves being outdoors, but I sometimes worry about how we live so close to the road."

Ben stepped forward to help Mary stand then popped open the door. He pulled a business card from his wallet and handed it to her. "You call me if you need anything, all right? I'm not that far away, and I'm pretty good with a hammer." He winked.

Chuckling, Mary turned and patted his cheek. "Thank you. I'll be in touch." She went inside and closed the door behind her.

Bella started down the steps toward the truck and climbed in before Ben could say anything. When he reached the vehicle, she swiped hard against her cheeks. Aw man, had she been crying? He longed to take her in his arms, but it would have been awkward pulling her across the center console. And maybe that's not what she needed anyway. She could be the type who needed space when upset.

"What do you really know about her, Ben?" His dad's voice flickered in his mind for a moment before Ben batted it away.

Starting the vehicle, Ben drove, on instinct pointing the truck north instead of the southern road that would take them home. Whether she said so or not, Bella had to be disappointed about the turn of events. Still, Mary had remembered something. She just needed to remember it again.

He should say something, encourage Bella. But every consolation he could think to offer stuck to the roof of his mouth.

Instead he sank his foot against the pedal and drove north. They passed the lighthouse that was about five miles out of town then kept on going. He may not know the best way to comfort her, but he'd try all the same.

Bella didn't question their destination. In fact, she gazed out the window, lost in her thoughts, until at last, her attention redirected onto him. "You were really good with Noah."

OK. She wanted to avoid the topic of her own feelings for the moment. No problem.

Ben shrugged. "I like kids. My littlest cousins are fun."

"I've never really been around children much." She quieted again.

"Do you want kids of your own someday?" Yeesh. The words just popped out. It was kind of a deep question to ask, more like fourth or fifth date material.

But maybe it was better to know up front, since he'd always pictured himself with a mini brood. Elena hadn't wanted children, but by the time they'd discussed the topic, he was already willing to compromise anything to be with her.

"I never really thought I did. But now . . . if it happened with the right guy, yeah. I think I'd like a family."

His chest flooded with all kinds of warmth. Ben wanted to look over at her, but he kept his eyes on the road. "Me too."

They drove into a gravel parking lot on top of a rocky overhang that looked across the ocean. The unmarked pull-off was so small it would be easy to miss if someone didn't know it existed. Tall seagrass on the cliff waved in the upward breeze. He keyed off the ignition and turned to face her.

"I guess I've always been sure I'd be a terrible mother." She bit her lip. "My example growing up wasn't the best."

"Maybe that's why you'll be a really good one."

"Huh." A small smile slid over her lips. "I like that perspective."

"Glad to hear it." After hopping out of the truck, he walked around the vehicle to open her door.

As if just noticing their surroundings, her nose scrunched while she climbed out. "Where are we?"

"Heart's Cove."

She quirked an eyebrow.

"Don't knock the name. I come here when I need to get away, to think. I thought you could use a little escape."

For a moment, she just stood there, staring at him. Then she stepped forward into his arms, so hard he nearly stumbled backward. He relished the feel of her against him.

She tilted her head up to gaze into his eyes. "I don't want to escape. Not everything, anyway." A pause. "I don't want to escape *this*."

His heart pumped hard against his chest.

Behind them, a couple walked up the hidden path from the cove toward the parking lot, laughing and interrupting the moment.

Ben leaned his head close, lowering his voice. "Neither do I. Now come on. I have something to show you."

How had Ben known exactly what she needed?

"Wow. This view is . . ." There weren't words for it, really. Bella stood on the precipice of a cliff next to Ben and gazed out over the water. A fifteen-foot arch of rock sheltered them from the sun.

Without pushing her to talk, he'd led her from the dirt-and-gravel parking lot down a path into this tiny cave of sorts. They'd walked through the cool rocky formation, which ended at the bluff.

"I know." Ben lowered himself to a sitting position, dangling his feet over the edge. About thirty feet below them the water crashed into foamy white waves against the cliff. "You should see it at sunset."

"I can only imagine." Careful not to slip on the loose pebbles and sand, Bella seated herself next to him. Her heart raced as she looked down.

Ben pointed to the left. "The beach is that way. We just have to backtrack through the cave and continue down the path we were on."

"We should check it out in a bit." She leaned her head on his shoulder. "But for now, I like it here just fine."

"We can stay here as long as you want."

"Much as I appreciate that, I shouldn't keep you from your work. You still have several hours of daylight left."

"Eh." Ben wove their fingers together and leaned his head against the top of hers. "I need a break anyway."

"Liar." But in this moment she couldn't gather the energy—or positivity—to leave this place of refuge and beauty. The meeting with Mary Robinson had deflated her in ways she hadn't thought possible. After all, until yesterday she'd never expected that she would find out about her father any other way than through Mom.

But then that tiny flicker of hope had seeped through the cracks of the walls she'd built up around her heart. And boom! They'd crashed down as if hit by a bulldozer.

"Hey." Ben's voice rumbled in her ear. "My mom texted me this morning and wanted me to extend an invitation to our next Baker family dinner. Guess you made quite an impression on everyone Friday night."

Seriously? Goosebumps slid along the edge of Bella's neck.

"They all made quite an impression on me too."

Ben snorted. "I'll bet."

"No, really. You have no idea how blessed you are to have family. And such a great one at that." She angled her head, pressing her cheek into the soft fabric of his T-shirt.

"I guess I do take it for granted sometimes." He turned her hand over and traced the palm lines with his thumb, sending shivers up her spine with the light touch. "Do you have any good memories with your mom?"

"Some. We were dirt-poor growing up because my mom was only twenty when I was born. She worked two, sometimes three jobs, to keep us off the street. We were poor but happy."

Bella smiled as a memory she hadn't thought about in forever surfaced. "For my sixth birthday, she somehow convinced the manager of a movie theater she cleaned to let us in two hours before the theater opened to watch the latest Disney movie. Mom even let me pick out a candy bar at the drugstore beforehand and popped a bag of popcorn. It was eight in the morning, and I got to eat chocolate and have my mom all to myself for a whole hour and a half."

"That sounds nice."

"It was. But three short years later, she forgot my birthday. She'd qualified for a scholarship at the local university and took night classes while continuing to work, and I never saw her anymore. I practically lived with my best friend and her family."

Ben's lips feathered a kiss against her temple. "I'm sure that was hard. But maybe she didn't completely fail you. Seems like you get your strength and determination from her."

The distant boom of the ocean below nearly drowned out his softly spoken words. He was trying to be sensitive but also maybe to challenge her to think differently about her mother and the choices she'd had to make back then.

Bella shook her head. "You're right in a way. My strength came from being forced to do life on my own, without family to support me. Because while my mom was off pursuing her dreams of a business empire, she ruined my own." Hot flashes shot through her veins.

Pushing backward, she stood and brushed off her shorts and the backs of her legs.

Ben rose and stuck his hands in his pockets. "Sorry. I didn't mean to push."

"It's fine. My backside was just getting numb."

His eyebrow quirked. "Right. Well, do you want to head home or visit the beach?"

What did it mean that she'd thought of the Iridescent Inn when he'd said *home*? She was spilling pieces of herself to him that only Jessica knew. Her heart was hemorrhaging all over the place.

Then why, instead of feeling ripped to shreds, did it beat with new intensity? Feel almost . . . whole?

Bella turned on her heels and strode through the cave, glancing back toward the parking lot. But the beach called to her, so she pivoted that way.

Ben caught up to her, and they walked down a series of steps until they emerged on an empty beach. The rocky face surged above them, cocooning them from everyone and everything outside of this sheltered bay.

After a few minutes of breathing in the tranquility, she turned to Ben, whose eyes followed the water in and out. Once again he was giving her the space she needed to process, to think, and it made her want to tell him all the more.

"You're probably wondering how my mom ruined my dreams."

"Only if you want to tell me."

"I do." She pressed a hand to her chest. "When I was a freshman in high school, I had the chance to go on a school trip to Europe. My dream was to travel and study history—that was my passion. Ironic, isn't it? The girl who didn't know her own history loved to learn the history of others."

"Makes sense, actually."

"I guess. Anyway, my mom said she'd show up for the meeting when everyone was to sign up and pay the deposit for the trip, but she never did. All the spots were filled. And she never even apologized, just said a meeting ran over. She'd started her own business and was doing all she could to make it a success."

Ben was quiet for a bit, his pursed lips a sure sign he was thinking. "So, did you end up studying history? I thought you had an MBA."

"My undergrad is in history, but I couldn't find a job after graduating. My mom offered me one at her company, and I don't know, I guess I thought maybe it was a chance for us to get closer. I pursued an MBA because she paid for it, and I ended up liking it too."

"But the two of you didn't get closer."

A seagull glided overhead, its squawk harsh against the peaceful setting.

"No. In fact, seeing who she's become, the things she'll do to get ahead, has made me even more determined to see if I can find my father. Well, not him, because he's dead, but his family, if he has any." Bella pushed an errant strand of hair behind her ear. "My mom and I are alike in some ways, but I don't want to be anything like her, really. Maybe if I know the rest of my history, who I really am, then I can figure out where I fit into this world."

Exhaustion weighed down her bones, and she sank onto the sand. Chucking off her sandals, Bella extended her legs in front of her.

Ben sat too. "I'm not sure what to say, Bella." He glanced at the sky, his face a mask of concentration. "I'd like to tell you that

I understand, but the truth is that I sometimes wish I didn't know all of my family history."

"What do you mean?" She tapped the side of his foot with her own, and he caressed the ridge of her foot with his big toe.

"Just that knowing everything your family has ever done— all the amazing things they've achieved—could mean you'll have a lot to live up to." He exhaled a deep breath. "When I was around ten years old, I overheard my grandpa tell my dad that 'we Bakers are the bedrock of this community. If we don't lead it, then who will?' And I know what he meant by that."

"What?"

"He equated leading with owning businesses in the town, and that's what all of my family before me has done so far. I'm the oldest Baker cousin, and it's up to me to lead the rest. But look at me. I'm about to lose my inn and disgrace the family name." He groaned and lay back against the sand.

She didn't hesitate to drop next to him, tucking herself against his body and settling her head into the crook of his arm. "If it happens, then losing the inn won't be your fault. You were handed something you didn't really want in the first place, something that was already on the rocks, and no one helped you."

"So? No one helped my dad start his business. Or my aunts. Or my uncle. They all pulled themselves up by their bootstraps and just did it somehow."

"The economy is different now. Things all around are different. You can't compare yourself to them."

"How can I not? I'll be the first Baker to fail." He sighed. "Even though I'm trying, I'm not the man they all want me to be. Maybe I'm not worthy of the Baker name."

"If the Baker name means kind and generous and smart and a little bit brooding and sexy as all get-out, then yeah. You are."

One arm still under her, he turned to prop himself up on his elbow so he could look down at Bella. His free hand found her waist, fingers grazing the bare skin of her hip where her shirt rode up just a bit. "You mean that?"

"Of course I do. Ben, you're incredible, and any family would be proud to claim you. Don't sell yourself short." Stretching out her hand, Bella traced the contours of Ben's face, his stubble rough under her fingertips.

Their eyes connected, and he lowered himself toward her, stopping just above her for the briefest of moments. Then his lips dipped and caught hers in the sweetest of kisses for one, two, three seconds before easing back and returning for something deeper, hungrier. Her body ignited, all synapses firing at his touch.

The applause of the ocean whooshed in her ears, overpowering any thought or doubt or anything beyond this moment, the intense flood of heat and emotion deluging her heart and body and mind.

She cradled his head between her hands as she matched his fiery kisses with her own. Ben fluttered kisses down her neck then worked his way upward to nip her earlobe until his lips returned to her mouth.

Finally, he pulled away, dropping back down beside her on the sand, both breathing heavily as they stared at the sky. Draping an arm across his chest, she fisted his shirt, and the scent of his deodorant lingered near her nose. Bella closed her eyes and prayed with all her might that Mary Robinson would remember something about the elusive Daniel and Camille.

Because after this—after the way he'd awakened something inside her that no one had ever touched—Bella didn't want to let go of Ben Baker.

But she didn't want to let go of her dream of a family either.

CHAPTER 9

A month ago Bella never would have imagined that she'd want to be at a Walker Beach festival.

Yet now she laughed as she stuck her face through a hole in a tall wooden cutout painted to look like two dancing olallieberries, a cross between a blackberry and raspberry. If she peeked to her right, she could just make out Ben's face poking through a similar hole.

The festival photographer held up a camera. "Say cheese."

Bella felt a pinch in her side. "Hey!"

"You aren't saying cheese."

"You didn't give me a chance." Bella turned her attention back to the photographer, grinned, and yelled, "Cheese!"

"Beautiful." Flashing them a thumbs-up, the photographer moved on, pivoting to snap shots of nearby vendor booths.

Bella stepped back from the cutout and found herself in Ben's arms.

He twirled her around and leaned down to give her a quick peck on the mouth. "I really like this side of you."

"And what side is that?" Pushing against his chest, she extricated herself from his grasp and shot him the sauciest look she could manage without laughing.

Ignoring the hordes of townspeople mingling all around them, Ben snuck his arms around her waist again. "The goofy side."

"Guess you bring it out in me." She exaggerated a sigh, unfolded her arms, and circled them around his neck.

"Either that or you're punchy from a lack of sleep." His eyebrows waggled.

She rolled her eyes but couldn't hide the grin on her lips. It was true—the last five days had been filled to the brim with everything but sleep. Many, many stolen kisses, lots of late-night dinners, and loads of time spent working together to start implementing Bella's limited "save the inn" plan had taken the place of rest.

In fact, other than the hoard of pushy texts and phone calls she'd received from her mom looking for an update, this had been the best week of Bella's life.

My patience is wearing thin, Bella. I'm running out of time to save this company. Are you going to come through for me or not? Mom's latest text message assaulted Bella's current happiness, sending a sobering shock through her body.

She took back what she'd thought earlier. Even more than the Olallieberry Festival in Walker Beach, she longed to go back to that secluded cove where it had been only her and Ben. No inns, no mothers, and no reminders that this was just tempo-rary—unless Bella somehow found a way to have everything she wanted.

Or the courage to choose.

"Where did my goofy girl go?" Ben's forehead met hers.

She forced a smile. "Back to reality."

Sighing, he let go of her waist and snagged her hand. They started walking down Main Street, which was blocked off to traffic south of the dual parking lots. "I'm sorry we haven't had time to investigate more into your dad's story. Last Bud told me, Mary hadn't remembered anything more. He's asked around, but no one else remembers your parents."

Booths lined either side of the street. Ben's aunts Jules and Louise shared a booth where they were selling their art and olive oils. Next to them, the local coffee and ice cream shop, Java's Village Bean, featured olallieberry ice cream, which Bella and Ben had sampled earlier. She could still taste the rich creaminess on her tongue.

Bella squeezed Ben's hand, trying to offer some reassurance. "Regardless of all that, I'm having a good time."

"I'm glad." Ben's eyes narrowed as he studied the street, looking from Carlotta Jenkins's clothing booth, which featured bright yellow scarves, flowing purple skirts, and everything in between, to the Frosted Cake's booth piled high with olallieberry pie offerings.

His gaze landed on a booth where a woman sat with a little girl who was dressing a pink baby doll. A silver-painted butterfly adorned the girl's cheek, and an artful arrangement of wine crates and stacked bottles decorated the table in front of them.

Ben tugged Bella that way. "Hello, ladies. How's it going?"

The brunette with the little girl shrugged. "Not as busy as usual. Normally I'm sold out by this time and taking mail orders, but today I still have fifty percent of my stock left."

"I wonder if Evan was right. He thinks the earthquake has tanked our tourism numbers."

Moving her hands through the little girl's curls, the woman pulled it back into a pair of pigtails. "Something is definitely different."

Ben shook his head and turned to Bella. "At the height of the festival, typically it's so crowded that you can hardly maneuver through the street."

"That's too bad."

The woman's eyes moved to Bella, lighting with interest. "Hi, I'm Heather, and this is my daughter, Mia."

"Bella." She leaned down to examine the wines, which were stamped with a Campbell Wines label. "Are these local?"

"Yes, from my family's vineyard up the road."

"I'll take a bottle of chardonnay, please." Bella reached into her purse and pulled out some cash. "Actually, make it two."

"Great." Heather nudged Mia off her lap and started packaging the first bottle. "How do you and Ben know each other? I'm his best friend's little sister."

"Evan?"

"No, Derek. He's not in town right now."

"Oh, right. Ben's mentioned him." After their time together on Monday, Ben had told her so much more about his life than the guarded man she'd first met. Bella had tried to match his level of openness but had held back certain details so he wouldn't discover the truth.

Every time she'd avoided a topic, pain had gripped the back of her throat, and she'd felt like the biggest jerk in the world.

It didn't matter what she'd told herself when she'd first come to town. She knew without a doubt that withholding or skirting the truth was just as bad as lying.

She handed Heather the money and took the bag with the wrapped bottles of wine. "Thank you."

"Of course."

Ben waved to his friend. "Tell your dad I say hello."

A shadow passed over Heather's face as she nodded. "I will."

They turned and continued their way down the street. Ben tried to buy Bella some flowers from a man named Lee Rivas at the Fleur de Lee booth, but she shook her head. "Then I wouldn't have a free hand to hold yours."

He conceded his defeat. But when he saw his cousin Shannon painting faces in the kids' area, a wicked gleam appeared in his eyes. "I think you should get a mule painted on your face."

"A mule?"

"Yeah, because you were so stubborn when we first met."

"Excuse me?" She stopped walking in the middle of the street. "*I* was stubborn? You were the one who would barely acknowledge my existence."

He grinned and pulled her close. "I had to protect myself."

"Because I was so vicious." Then she made a face and arched back against his hold. "And wait, did you really just compare me to a mule?"

"A really, really cute one."

A laugh burst from her lips, and she wiggled out of his hold. "You're going to have to make up for that one later, bub."

He sidled up next to her and leaned down to whisper in her ear. "I look forward to the challenge."

Bella pushed him away with a grin and strode toward Shannon, who was busy painting a little boy's face. As they moved closer, she recognized Noah Robinson. His grandma stood off to one side fanning herself despite the gorgeous seventy-degree weather.

All three looked their way as Bella and Ben approached.

Shannon smiled. "How are you guys?"

Noah's eyes widened, and he leaped from the seat, running to Ben. He pulled on Ben's shorts until Ben leaned down so Noah could whisper something in his ear.

"Noah, don't bother the nice man." His grandmother stepped forward.

"He's not bothering me." Ben straightened and patted Noah's curls. "You did an excellent job on your mission, little man. Helped to save the world with your reading, in fact."

Noah's small chest puffed. He turned and ran back to the seat next to Shannon, who resumed painting his face with tiger stripes.

Mary shook her head. "That's nice of you, but I've told him not to talk to strangers without asking first."

Strangers? Bella faced the older woman. "Mary, I'm Bella, and this is Ben. Remember? We visited you earlier this week."

Shannon's chin jerked toward them, her paintbrush smearing black across a ribbon of orange on Noah's cheek.

Mary's hands fluttered as she let loose a stilted laugh. "Oh yes. Of course. Nice to see you again." She wandered to the booth next door to peruse some homemade candles.

"Is it just me, or does it seem like she doesn't remember us?" Bella kept her voice low so Mary wouldn't hear but Shannon and Ben would.

"I'm Noah's preschool teacher, so I see more than most." Shannon stroked Noah's curls. He snuggled against her, smearing paint on her shirt, but Ben's cousin didn't seem to mind in the slightest. "Her memory is definitely getting worse."

And *this* was the person who held Bella's fate—the fate of her relationship with Ben—in her hands.

"Excuse me for a minute. I'll be right back." Bella shoved the bag of wine into Ben's arms and hurried down a sidewalk that led to the beach. Standing on the edge of the boardwalk, she breathed in the fresh beach air, willing her heart rate to slow, trying to take in the inevitable news about Mary's memory— and what it meant for Bella.

"Bella, I'm glad I caught you."

Briefly closing her eyes, she tried to pretend she hadn't heard Lisa Baker's voice. But then the woman was standing beside her, and she couldn't ignore it anymore. Pasting a smile on her face, she turned to greet Ben's mom. "Hi, Lisa. How are you?"

Today the woman looked effortless in a white sleeveless top that accentuated her toned, tan arms. Of the two siblings, Ashley most resembled their mother, but Bella could see Ben in his mom's nose, lips, and chin. "I'm . . . good."

Bella tilted her head. "I sense a but."

Slowly, Lisa nodded. "It's good to see Ben so happy. You bring that out in him. We've all noticed it. His burden was so heavy, his heart broken, before you came along." Her sharp appraisal raked over Bella before she sighed. "I know it's not my place at all, and he'd be unhappy with me if he knew I was talking to you, but as his mom, I worry. I don't want him to get hurt again."

Oh, kill her now. "I don't want that either."

"I'm glad to hear it." Quick as lightning, Lisa grabbed Bella's hand and clutched it to her chest. "I haven't known you long, but I sense you're a good person. Not malicious, so you'd never hurt him intentionally, not like Elena did. Still, if you have any doubts, then maybe . . . just consider what he's been through."

Bella swallowed hard against her aching throat.

"But"—Lisa smiled, her eyes radiating true sweetness—"if things work out between the two of you, I'll welcome you with open arms into our family."

A hot tear trailed down Bella's cheek. She swatted it away, but Lisa's knowing gaze revealed she'd seen it.

"Thank you." Bella managed to croak the words out.

"Well." Lisa pulled her into a quick hug then backed up. "I've said my piece. I hope you enjoy the rest of the festival." She turned on her heel and walked away.

And Bella took off at a sprint down the beach.

What was she doing, continuing this charade?

Falling to her knees onto the warm sand, she fumbled to pull her phone from her purse and dialed Jessica. When she got her best friend's voicemail, words just tumbled free. "Jess, it's me. I . . . I don't know what to do. I've been lying to Ben, and I think that maybe he's someone I could love, but he doesn't know who I am. And, Jess, other than a big fat liar, *I* don't even know who I am, and I probably never will. Never. Help. Tell me what to do."

Then she dropped her phone, put her head in her hands, and allowed the tears to come.

CHAPTER 10

$\mathcal{T}$he decking was coming along. If only Ben could say the same for his relationship with Bella.

"You and Bella seemed pretty cozy at the festival on Saturday." Evan moved the ladder to the next rail post on the upper porch decking of the inn, while Ben snagged the drill from the ground.

Ben climbed the tall ladder that Evan held steady, stopping when he reached the bottom of the second-story porch. "Were you there? I didn't see you." Aiming the tool at the wood, he drilled two clearance holes so he could reinforce the posts.

After finishing the roof last week, he'd started repairing damaged floorboards on the decking and by tonight, Tuesday evening, he'd moved on to fixing the wobbly posts. Next, he just needed to reseal and stain the deck, repair the broken staircase, and throw some paint on the walls. With the exception of the guest rooms in the north wing, he'd then be back in business.

Or so he hoped. He still needed customers. But Bella was working on that.

"I was helping in Chrissy's store the whole time. She couldn't get off the couch." Evan's voice drifted upward on the cool evening breeze. "Everyone kept stopping in to ask after her, so I didn't even make it outside for some pie."

Setting the drill on the top of the ladder, Ben pulled a half-inch carriage bolt and hammer from his tool belt. "I heard she made a turn for the worst. I'm sorry. It must be rough to see her like that."

"Yeah." The ragged word was tinged with grief.

Ben tapped in the bolt, shimmed it, and installed a nut and washer. Then he repeated the action with the second hole, tightening the nut until the bolt head was flush against the post. He'd check everything with a level in a bit. Tools back in his belt and drill collected, Ben lowered himself to the ground.

Evan leaned against the bottom post supporting the decking above, eyes staring in the distance. The sun had nearly met the horizon. Time to call it a day.

"You want a Coke?"

"Sure."

Ben walked toward the workshop on the north side of the inn where he kept his tools and a mini-fridge. He entered the dank space and put away his tools. Popping open the fridge, cold blasted his fingers as he grabbed two sodas.

He returned to his friend and held out a Coke.

"Thanks." Taking the red can, Evan popped the top and took a swig.

Ben did the same, the fizz of carbonation and the shot of sugar just what he needed at the end of another long day of physical labor. Turning, he took in the sight of his family's inn, his legacy. Weeks of hard work had paid off. If he could get his finances in order, if Bella's plan really worked, then maybe he could make his family proud.

"Ben, you're incredible and any family would be proud to claim you." Bella's life-giving words from that day more than a week ago in Heart's Cove drifted back to him. She'd been so confident, not a flicker of doubt.

He'd liked how he looked in her eyes.

And yet . . .

"So, you and Bella are getting pretty serious, then?"

Ben turned to find his friend's eyes on him as Evan sipped from his can. "I don't know. Maybe."

He'd thought so but something had happened at the festival. He'd attributed it to their meet up with Mary Robinson. The news that Mary might never remember Bella's parents had upset her. Bella had even run off for a good half hour in the middle of their date.

But on Sunday, she'd stayed in her room all day claiming a headache. Had even begged off Baker family dinner, which she'd agreed to attend. He'd skipped too, taking the opportunity to work on the inn again.

But even yesterday and today, she'd hardly been around. He missed her.

He and Evan walked to the gate separating the inn from the beach. Ben popped it open and walked through, his gaze raking over the waves far below. "I think she may be avoiding me." Continuing their jaunt, they sauntered toward a bluff to the left. Here the wind was stronger, cooling the sweat clinging to his body.

"Why would she do that, man?"

"Not sure. I thought we were good. Really good." He drained the rest of his Coke. The dregs bit into his tongue. "Maybe this is just how she gets when she's focused, though. She's helping me with my business plan."

Evan was quiet for a bit. "Or maybe she's preparing to leave."

"She hasn't mentioned that."

"Come on, dude. She doesn't live here. She has a life in the city. And she was never planning to stay past a few weeks, right?" His buddy frowned. "Have you talked about what happens when she goes home? LA isn't that far, but long distance is rough. Or so I hear."

Ben's jaw tensed, and he moved his gaze toward the long waving grass overtaking the bluff. "No, we haven't. It's all so new."

"And you want to be careful after Elena. I get that."

"She's different than Elena."

"Are you sure?" At Ben's quick head swivel, Evan held up his hands in defense. "Hey, man, I like her. She seems great. But what if she's avoiding you because she's hiding something? I mean, do you know that much about her?"

Ben's fingers pressed into the aluminum can. First Dad, now Evan. "Why does everyone keep asking me that?"

"Because we care."

Striding to the edge of the cliff, Ben allowed the ocean's roar to fill the void of peace left by Evan's question. "I may not know her favorite color or her favorite food or even her middle name. But we've talked about deeper stuff. The details that matter. Isn't that more important?"

"Sure. As long as you think you can trust her."

"Of course I can." He trusted the way she'd looked when she'd talked about her mom, the hurts she'd endured, the reasons she wanted so desperately to find her dad.

You trusted Elena too.

No. Elena had been a liar who had fooled him from the beginning. She'd used Ben for her own benefit, and when she'd gotten what she wanted from him, she had spit him out.

Maybe she'd been planning to leave all along.

Knowing Bella as he did now, Ben couldn't believe he'd ever seen any resemblance between the two women.

"I'm not sure what is going on with her." Wind whipped Ben's cheeks, stinging them with its intensity. "Maybe she's distracted by the search for her dad. Maybe she's trying to figure out what's happening between us. But do I believe she's hiding something? No way."

She can't be. I'd see it.

The ocean receded, its silence deafening his ears.

~

"I'm sorry, Bella." Bud Travis scratched his ear as he picked up a can of green beans. "I've been racking my brain but just can't think of any more leads."

"Oh." Bella tilted her head down and frowned.

A few scuffs marked the concrete floors of the modern Hardings Market, where she'd followed Bud after spotting him from her seat at the Frosted Cake's back window. Shannon and Ashley had understood when she'd left halfway through dinner to chase him down.

She'd never be that rude on a regular basis, but ever since she'd encountered Mary Robinson and Lisa Baker, she'd been trying to get in touch with Bud. According to Carlotta Jenkins— the woman had proven useful after all—he'd been out of town visiting his son and grandkids, and he rarely answered his cell phone.

The man ran his finger along the top of the green can decorated with dancing vegetables. "I'll keep thinking, but no one I've asked so far remembers Camille Miranda."

Did she dare reveal her mom's real name? What would he think of her?

But this might be her only shot at finding her dad's family without Mom's help. And she could only get so far on half-truths. "What about . . . Camille Moody?" Bella bit her lip so hard she thought it might bleed, praying Bud wouldn't scold her too hard for giving false information.

"Camille Moody?" The man's bushy eyebrows lifted. "Isn't that the name of the developer trying to buy land here?"

That's right. Ben had said Bud was a city councilman. They'd probably been informed of Mom's intentions.

Sweat tickled Bella's upper lip. "Um. Yes."

Bud put the green beans back on the wooden shelf and narrowed his eyes at her. "Young lady, just what are you up to? Because I'll have you know that Ben Baker is a fine man, and if you're playing with him—"

"I'm not. I promise." Bella glanced around, but no other grocery store customers headed down their aisle. "I just need to know. I really am. . ." She blew out a frustrated breath.

A hand gripped her shoulder, squeezing gentler than she deserved.

She dragged her gaze back to Bud, surprised to find compassion staring back at her.

"I don't know your story, Bella, and maybe that's for the best. But I do know that a relationship built on lies won't last."

Her jaw ached from clenching her teeth too hard. "I know." A pause. "Are you going to tell Ben who I really am?"

The man studied her good and long. The sound of beeping registers drifted from the front of the store, filling in the silence between them. Bud crossed his arms over his chest. "I won't insert myself where I don't belong, but I won't lie if I'm asked."

"Fair enough." Then, because this wasn't a business transaction after all, Bella softened her voice. "Thank you. For everything. I really am here to find out about my dad."

Bud nodded. "Glad to hear it. But I'm afraid knowing the real last name probably won't change anything. Only Mary mentioned knowing any couple by the first names of Camille and Daniel. Doesn't mean the truth isn't out there, though."

Maybe not. But it could take her a long time to find it.

Time she didn't have.

With a quick goodbye, Bella turned and started the mile-long trek back to the inn. She hoped Ben wouldn't be there. She'd avoided him the last few days by staying in her room or leaving before the sun was up, when he usually started his work for the day.

She knew if he asked, she couldn't keep lying to him.

But she wasn't ready to tell the truth.

She wasn't ready to lose him.

Walking in the growing darkness, not even the fresh air bolstered her. When she returned to the inn, she hurried to her room where a light shone beneath the door. Had she forgotten to turn it off this morning? Cautiously pulling her key card from her purse, Bella entered the room.

"Finally."

Bella squeaked at the voice but quickly recovered upon seeing the brunette seated on her bed. "Jess?"

"In the flesh." Her best friend leaped from the bed, enveloping Bella in a hug.

Fresh tears welled up in Bella's eyes. Goodness. What was wrong with her? It hadn't been that long since she'd seen Jessica. Still, her throat flashed hot. "What are you doing here?"

Her friend pulled back from the hug, studying Bella from behind her purple cat-eye glasses. "I just got your message this morning. I was camping with some friends for a long weekend and didn't have cell service. By the time we got home late last night, I showered and sank into bed and didn't bother to check my messages."

Jessica had always been there for Bella exactly when she needed her. She was the closest thing to a sister Bella had had growing up, and she'd continued to be loyal in all the ways that counted. Still, the last time they'd talked, Bella hadn't embraced that loyalty or her friend's heartfelt advice. "I wondered."

"Yep, and as soon as I got your message, I made sure I didn't have any last-minute appointments." Jess was a hairdresser out of her apartment in Burbank. "I can stay for a few days."

Sniffing away any trace of potential tears, Bella straightened and strode into the room, plopping onto the desk chair facing the bed. "You could have just called, you know."

Jessica retook her position on the bed, a wary look on her face. "I thought you may need more than that." She pulled a plastic bag off the bedside table and shook loose a few candy bars, Twizzlers, and a bag of chili cheese Fritos. "For instance, a phone call couldn't have delivered these."

"You're a saint. My waistline doesn't thank you, but I do." Bella held up a hand, and Jessica tossed her a Snickers bar.

"Always happy to oblige." Jess ripped open the bag of chips, sending the scent of spicy corn floating through the room. "By the way, I booked the room across the hall, but Ben was nice enough to let me into yours. He's quite a hottie." Quirking an eyebrow, she crushed a chip between her teeth.

Bella focused on unwrapping her chocolate bar. The top rippled with hidden peanuts that crunched as she took a bite. "Yes, he is."

"And? What's going on there?"

Any pleasure the chocolate should have provided fled from Bella's tongue, replaced with a bitterness that came from the sour turning of her stomach. Sighing, she lowered the Snickers. "Not a whole lot."

"Sounded like a whole lot."

"I should clarify. Not a whole lot anymore."

Crunch, crunch, crunch. "Explain." Jessica wiped her fingers on the edge of the plastic bag.

Bella rummaged in her desk, located a napkin, and tossed it to her friend. "There's not much to the story. As you know, I came here under false pretenses, though I never actually told a mistruth."

"Which is still lying."

Being outspoken herself, Bella appreciated Jess's forthrightness.

Most of the time.

Today, it rubbed raw a tender spot in her soul.

"I know that now, yes." Bella's fingers fidgeted as she messed with the empty candy wrapper. She explained the rest of the story to her friend, who reserved any more words until she was done.

"And so I've come to an impasse. I want to help him, to be with him, but I'm not naive enough to believe we can have any sort of real future if I don't tell him the truth. The problem is, if I tell him the truth, he won't sell, and I'll give up the only shot I have at finding my dad. If I *don't* tell him the truth and *do* convince him to sell, I'll lose him when he discovers it afterward, which he's bound to do."

Somehow she'd managed to keep her voice steady during her explanation, but it quavered as she presented her last choice —the worst one of the bunch. "And if I risk telling him the truth, and he hates me for it, I'll lose everything. He won't sell, Mom won't tell me about Dad, and I'll lose Ben too. Both things I want will be gone forever."

Crumpling the candy wrapper, she tossed it in the trash. It left smudges of chocolate on her palm that she wiped away with a napkin. "Logically, I should choose the scenario that at least guarantees I get one of them. But emotionally . . ."

Pursing her lips together, Jessica rolled the chip bag closed and set it on the side table again. "I think you know what you have to do, Bells. And logic has nothing to do with it."

Pulling up her legs onto the chair, Bella wrapped her arms around them and set her face into the crack between her knees. She groaned. "I know. But I'm so afraid of reliving what happened with Jake in high school." That had taken her months to get over. And her feelings for Ben were a million times more intense, more real.

Jessica leaned forward. "Bella, that was completely different. Jake Merrick was an immature boy who couldn't handle the truth."

Immature or not, Bella had been half in love with Jake the day they'd met during the regional academic decathlon tournament her senior year. He'd impressed her with his intelligence, his confidence in his plans for the future. He might have lived an hour away from her, but for a whole month after they met, they'd talked on the phone late into the night about anything and everything. Jake was candid about how his dad had grown depressed after losing his job a year before and his parents' subsequent divorce.

"I realize there are differences." Bella's arms tightened around her knees. "But don't you see the similarities too? He didn't want me anymore once he found out I was a Moody."

She still remembered the day they'd realized the "witch" who had fired Jake's dad and sent his whole family spiraling into chaos was none other than Camille Moody. Still remembered how it felt for Jake to stand her up for prom a week later.

Bella swallowed hard. "And it'll be the exact same thing with Ben."

"You can't compare the situations. The outcome with Jake was in no way your fault. Just a strange and crazy coincidence. This time, it's a mess of your own making."

Bella flinched at Jessica's candid words. "It still doesn't change the facts. I'm a Moody, and when Ben finds out he isn't going to want anything to do with me."

"If that happens, it'll be because you lied, not because of your last name."

Bella released her legs, her feet landing square on the carpet, hands clenching into fists at her side. "He would have sent me packing that first day if he'd associated me with Mom. Face it— I'm Bella Moody, and I can't escape all the connotations that brings."

"Girl." Jess climbed off the bed and squatted in front of Bella. "You are *not* the sum of your name, so you have to stop acting like it defines you. If Ben is supposed to be in your life, he'll forgive you, you'll be together, and it won't have a single thing to do with who your parents are. Only who *you* are, deep down."

And that was Bella's greatest fear.

CHAPTER 11

*T*he bank was the last place in the world where Ben wanted to be.

But he didn't have a choice.

Ben glanced up and down Main Street, but no one seemed to notice him as he strode closer to Walker Beach First Bank. Of course, that didn't mean that Aunt Kiki couldn't see him from her shop across the way, but there were lots of reasons people went to the bank. Not that everyone who went wore a tie, though. Why had he worn the stupid thing in the first place?

Whatever Matthew wanted to talk to him about, Ben's wearing or not wearing a tie wasn't going to change it.

Shaking out his hands, Ben pushed open the double doors of the bank and breezed through. Pleasant elevator music and a piney scent greeted him, and his feet sank into the plush blue carpet. A handful of tellers standing behind a high glossy counter helped the Thursday afternoon rush of customers before a long summer weekend—one of the last before kids started a new school year. In open cubicles on the other side of the large room, several loan officers and advisors chatted on their phones, drank their coffee, or worked on their computers.

No one seemed to notice him enter, which suited Ben just fine.

Passing a water dispenser with cone-shaped cups set up in front, he slipped down the back hall toward Matthew's office, where his former football teammate had asked Ben to meet at four-thirty. When he reached the large oak door, he knocked.

"Come in."

Ben blew out a breath, pasted on a smile, and barged into the office.

It didn't matter how large the office was—with his stacked frame and broad shoulders, Matthew Lulich looked a bit ridiculous hunched over his computer. He glanced up then stood, extending a hand from behind the desk. "Ben, good to see you."

Striding forward, Ben took Matt's hand in a firm grip and shook. "Same." Nearly choking on the lie, he looked the bank manager in the eyes, searching for the reason he'd called him in. But the man revealed nothing.

"Have a seat, man. And have some candy." Matthew indicated the bowl of Warheads on his desk.

Ben lowered himself into the plush chair across the desk, keeping his shoulders straight. "I'm OK."

"I appreciate you coming in on such short notice."

"No problem. Don't want to bite the hand that feeds me and all that." Ben attempted a laugh then cringed at the strangled noise that came from his mouth.

Matthew glanced at the clock ticking away the seconds on the wall to Ben's right before he rolled the sleeves of his expensive shirt to his elbows. He drew his lips into a frown. "There's no easy way to say this, so I'll just be straight with you. Dad found out that I've been giving you grace on your loan."

Unlike Ben, Matthew had been destined for bigger things than the family business—had even been recruited to the Arizona Cardinals his sophomore year of college at the University of Southern California. But a knee injury his first season had blown him all the way back to Walker Beach, where he'd stepped in to help his dad run the one and only local bank.

Ben didn't like where this was going. Norman Lulich wasn't a jerk, but he wasn't all that understanding of people who defaulted on their loans. That was Ben's reasoning for first coming to Matthew when he'd realized he might not make his payment that first month. His friend had promised they'd work with him, that he'd get in touch if anything changed. It had been months since Ben had heard anything.

He swallowed hard, wishing he'd snagged a cup of water on the way in. "You'll have to tell him thank you for me." Ben hated for his old buddy to understand just how desperate of a situation he was currently in, but the sympathy card might be his only play. "Things have been rough since I took over the inn. I think I'm finally starting to get on my feet, though."

"I'm glad to hear that. Because . . ." Matthew cleared his throat. "Sorry, man, I hate this."

Dread churned Ben's stomach. "Just say it."

"Dad said I needed to serve you with a notice of default." The man swiveled in his chair toward his computer, snatched a file folder, and turned back, sliding it across the desktop to Ben. "It's all in there. You have ninety days to catch up on your loans plus some fees and interest that have accrued."

Ben reached for the folder and opened it, his fingertips numb as he flipped through to the last page. His breath caught as he spied the number at the bottom—the amount he owed by November fourth. He shut his eyes to the amount that seemed so far out of his reach at the moment.

Unless Bella's tactics worked to draw in more customers or the grant Evan was still looking into panned out, he was doomed. He really would have no choice but to sell. And he knew just who would be waiting in the wings.

Moody Development.

He'd ruin his family's legacy and Walker Beach's vibe in one fell swoop. Bella had said it wouldn't be his fault, but Ben knew the truth.

Scrubbing a hand down his face, he reopened his eyes. "Is there any way we can talk about this? Can I meet with your dad? See if he'll flex once he's heard about my circumstances?"

"Normally I'd say yes, but we've had a bunch of people in the last few weeks asking for new loans or loan extensions." Matthew fidgeted with his tie. "The earthquake really did a number on a lot of businesses in town."

Heat flushed Ben's body. "So, your dad is just taking advantage of us?"

"Hey now." Matthew's nostrils flared, a flash of the old football player coming back to life.

"Sorry. That was out of line." Ben tugged at his collar. Oh, hang it. He loosened and removed his tie then stuffed it into his pocket.

"I know this is hard, man. Believe me, I tried to change his mind." Matthew rubbed the back of his neck. "He's actually granting a lot of people grace, but he said you defaulted before the earthquake, and you've had months to get your finances back on track. He wasn't feeling as generous with your situation."

His friend's cheeks grew red beneath his five o'clock shadow. Dude had probably taken the brunt of his dad's wrath for letting Ben off the hook as long as he had.

It was time to face the music. Ben wasn't going to get any help here.

He was on his own.

Bella's beautiful face flashed in his mind, her eyes filled with an unwavering belief in him. The band around his lungs eased. Yeah, things had been a bit slower between them this week, especially yesterday with her friend Jessica in town. He and Bella had hardly spent any time together except to review some ads messaging she was placing online.

They might not have had an opportunity to define what they meant to each other or even go on another date, but one thing was for certain—she was working behind the scenes to support him. And with a brilliant woman like Bella Miranda on his side, he wouldn't fail. Couldn't.

And . . . so what if he did?

For the first time, he allowed himself to wonder—would it be so bad if he lost the inn?

Embarrassing? Sure. But detrimental? Who knew. Maybe it would free him up to follow Bella back to LA. Not that he really wanted to leave Walker Beach. It was home, after all, and he'd always been OK with that. But there was something about Bella that felt like home too. Something indefinable that he couldn't put his finger on but knew was there.

Shutting the default notice into the folder and snapping it up, Ben thanked Matthew and practically ran out the bank's front doors. He hauled himself toward the Main Street east parking lot and into his truck. Might break the speed limit getting home but he had to find her.

Yeah, he needed to update her on the notice of default and get her thoughts on ramping up their efforts to save the inn. But the more pressing need was to push away any lingering doubts and take her in his arms and kiss her senseless.

To tell her what he knew he wanted, even more than saving his inn—the chance to explore a future with her.

These could be Bella's last moments at the Iridescent Inn.

Holding tightly to the stapled stack of papers in her hand, she leaned against the newly secured railing on the upper outside deck and breathed in the scent of the sea that floated toward her from the beach. The top of the stairs was still closed off with caution tape, but otherwise the decking was like new.

Despite the lingering odor of sealant and wood stain, which Ben had applied yesterday, there was nowhere in the whole world she'd rather be right now.

Except for Ben's arms.

But that might never happen again. Not after she told him the truth.

After about a day and a half together, Jessica had left early this morning, and Bella had taken the rest of the day to finish the business plan—the full version, no ideas held back—for Ben's inn. She'd completed it an hour ago and printed it for easier perusal. When she'd looked for Ben afterward, he was nowhere to be found. Then she remembered he'd mentioned in passing an appointment at the bank.

So for now, she waited.

For the hundredth time, Bella angled her head toward the parking lot, but her Lexus was still the only vehicle there. Huffing, she retreated through the sliding glass door on the deck into the upstairs lobby with its cozy couches and fireplace where Ben and Bella had shared their first pizza.

Still, however cozy, Ben's grandparents clearly hadn't updated the place since the 1980s. In her business plan, Bella had suggested modernizing first, including trading the wall-to-wall shaggy carpet for cost-effective but gorgeous laminate flooring and the gold wallpaper border along the ceiling for crown molding, which Ben could easily and inexpensively do himself. Together, they could make this place amazing.

If only he'd forgive her.

Her fingers crushed the business plan in her hands, wrinkling the first page.

She sighed. Whether Ben forgave Bella for her lies or not, she would leave the plan with him, giving him full access to her thoughts on how to save his inn. He deserved that and so much more from her.

And, yeah, maybe she'd never know who her father was or

discover if she had a family out there somewhere. But at least she'd have done the right thing. And with that, maybe Ben would see past her indiscretion.

Maybe she'd finally found somewhere to belong, with people who didn't see her as a Moody but just as Bella.

Sinking onto the couch closest to the fireplace, which afforded her a peek at the ocean from the window, Bella placed the plan on the coffee table. Upon second thought, she moved a vase over it so he wouldn't see it before she was ready to introduce it into the conversation. She itched to go over the details with him but knew she might not get that chance. Jessica had urged her to tell him the truth about who she was sooner rather than later. As usual, her best friend was right.

Bella had her bags packed, just in case.

"Hey."

Ben's voice jarred her from her thoughts, and she looked up at his approach. Oh, he was handsome in his slacks and button-down collared shirt, the edge of a tie peeking out from his pocket. There was no denying he filled out the ensemble in a handsome way, his biceps bulging beneath the blue fabric.

Her eyes drifted upward, connecting with his gaze as he moved closer. "Hi."

"What are you doing in here?" Ben slid onto the couch next to her, bringing with him a new scent. Was he wearing cologne? She couldn't help but lean toward him, savoring notes of sandalwood, patchouli, and orange.

Couldn't the man be all sweaty like usual? That would have made it a lot easier to drop the bomb she was about to unleash.

Yeah, right. Who was she kidding? He was sexy even after a day of working on the inn. Something about that construction worker vibe apparently did it for her.

Or maybe it was just Ben.

Her heart twisted.

Yes. Definitely just Ben.

"Waiting for you. I need to . . . I need to talk to you about something." She paused, noting a folder in his hands. "How did it go at the bank?"

"Terrible, actually." Ben waved the folder. "They served me with a notice of default. I have three months to pay what I owe, including fees and interest, or I can kiss this place goodbye." Instead of hitching, his voice reported the turn of events as facts with no emotional bearing on him.

"I'm so sorry." Bella placed a hand on his arm then tilted her head. "But you don't sound all that upset."

And there was the expected frown, but it only stayed on his lips for a moment. "Not gonna lie. It's upsetting. But I realized something."

"What's that?"

Ben set the folder next to him then angled his body toward Bella, placing one hand on her knee and the other over the back of the couch. He caught a strand of her hair in his fingers and rubbed it in circles.

She relished this. She'd missed this.

But everything was about to change.

He sighed. "I have been working so hard to save this inn, without even questioning if it's what I want. I'm not saying I'm against it. I think if I'd had some time to get used to the idea, to study the market, to understand the best way to run an inn, then maybe I would like it."

"From what you've told me, it was trial by fire."

"Right. And of course, there's the whole this-inn-has-been-in-my-family-for-generations thing." A squeeze to her knee. "That's not insignificant."

"No." Where was he going with this?

Her scrunched nose and squint must have given away her question because Ben smiled in reply. "But what I realized is that losing the inn wouldn't be the worst thing in the world."

"It wouldn't?" Her voice squeaked, and Bella cleared her throat. "What do you mean?"

Ben scooted closer, pulling her so near that her hands found their way around his neck. No, no, no. She needed to tell him. Now. But she was too intrigued, too hopeful. If he didn't care as much about losing his inn, what did that mean? For them?

He lowered his face so their noses touched tip to tip. "The worst thing in the world would be letting you leave without telling you how much you have come to mean to me. Bella, I know things haven't been the same between us this week, and I'm not sure why. I want to know what's going on in that head of yours. But even more, I need you to know what's going on in mine."

It hurt too much to look at him. She squeezed her eyes shut. *Tell him.* But his words—they were intoxicating. And her lips trembled, longing to feel him close the gap, longing to forget the lies dangling between them.

"Bella, I want—"

"Well, no wonder my calls have gone unanswered."

Bella tore away from Ben's embrace, her eyes searching for the disembodied voice, landing on the petite woman in a pantsuit standing at the top of the stairs.

What was Mom doing here?

This had to be a nightmare. Bella pinched the skin on her forearm but no such luck.

Ben turned. When he caught sight of her mother, he straightened and stood. "Hi. Can I help you?"

"I certainly hope so." Mom strode toward them in her black Prada heels, nose lifted slightly, her deep brown hair pulled back in a severe bun at the nape of her neck.

Rubbing the underside of his forearm, Ben glanced between Bella and Mom. "I'm not sure I understand. Were you looking for a place to stay?"

The air had thinned. This wasn't happening. Mom was going

to ruin everything, just like she always did. Of course, irony of ironies, this time because she'd actually shown up.

"I'm not here as a guest but as a future owner." Hand outstretched, Mom reached them. "Camille Moody, Moody Development."

Bella cringed.

Any warmth left drained from Ben's face. "Ah, Ms. Moody in the flesh. You just don't know when to give up, do you?"

"I overheard you saying you're not opposed to losing the inn anymore, and after hearing about your financials, I think you're making a wise decision."

"Wait. What?" His eyebrows squished together. "How long were you standing there spying on us?"

"Long enough. Spying is a Moody specialty." Mom directed her wry grin at Bella.

What was she doing? Bella gave a quick shake of her head, but Mom didn't notice.

Or just didn't care.

"And what did you say about my financials?" Ben stepped slightly in front of Bella, as if to protect her from this crazy woman.

He has no idea. Oh, she might throw up.

He continued. "I've told you over and over, and I'll tell you again—I'm not interested in selling to your company. I could give you myriad reasons, but right now it's simply because I don't like you. I want nothing to do with the Moody name."

A cruel laugh barked from Mom's throat. "Nothing? That's not what you were saying a few minutes ago." Her words hung in the air. She turned her eyes back to Bella once more. "Bella? Why don't you fill your *friend* in on the truth?"

Ben whipped around. "What's she talking about?"

Licking her lips, Bella swallowed hard. Forced through the dreaded words. "Ben, this is my mom."

"Your—" He backed up a step. "What does that mean?"

"It means, Mr. Baker, that my daughter was here to convince you to sell. But it appears that instead you've convinced *her* to forget who she really is and what's really important." Mom pulled an envelope from the oversized purple Coach purse hanging from her shoulder and extended it toward Ben, who had pivoted so he could keep them both in his sights.

It all appeared to be happening in slow motion.

"What's that?"

"This, Mr. Baker, is another official offer, which I've upped by 10 percent. You have to sign by Sunday at midnight or it's rescinded." Tapping the envelope against her palm, Mom tilted her head, eyes glinting. "And my next offer, if there is one, won't be so generous. Although if the financials my daughter told me about are anything remotely close to accurate, you won't be in business in a month or two. Which means you'll be kicking yourself for not accepting."

"The financials she told you about?"

Bella wanted to go to him, to put her arms around his neck, to reassure him of her affection with a kiss. But she stayed rooted where she stood. "Ben, I can explain."

Ben ignored her and crossed his arms as he narrowed his gaze at the envelope. "I. Am. Not. Interested."

Rolling her eyes, Mom set the offer on the arm of the couch closest to her. "For now. But I look forward to hearing from you once you've seen past your pride to what is practical." She looked at Bella. "I assume you don't need a ride back to the city?"

"As if I'd go anywhere with you right now." Bella's insides were on fire, a potent mixture of anger, regret, and overwhelming grief threatening to burn her to the ground.

"Fine. But I expect to see you at work on Monday." With a final nod, Mom turned on her heel and trounced down the stairs.

A few moments later, the front door of the inn slammed.

"Ben—"

"You were sent here to spy on me?" He ground out his words, his look searing her with its intensity.

Bella bit her lip. She could blame Mom, but the truth was the truth. "Yes."

Throwing up his hands, Ben strode to the door that led out to the deck.

She hurried after him. The sight of him gripping the railing, knuckles white, triceps flexed, nearly stopped her, but she managed to make it back to his side. "I'm so sorry, Ben. I really did come to find my dad. That was my price for convincing you to sell. Mom is the only one with the information I need, and I wanted that information more than anything."

"So, it was all a lie?"

"No!" The breeze turned into a wind, whipping her hair around her face. "I mean, yes, it started out that way, but everything else between us was real. My feelings for you. What I told you about myself, about my family."

He remained silent, his attention still on the sea.

Maybe he was hearing her. She continued. "If you'd told me a month ago, I'd never have believed it. But for the first time, I feel like I belong somewhere. Here in Walker Beach. Here with you." Bella placed her hand on his upper arm with a tentative touch.

Ben stiffened and moved away from her. Fire flashed in his eyes, and his cheeks drained of color. "What I can't believe is that I trusted another liar." His voice was ragged. "You must have thought I was a fool every time I told you something private. Every time I kissed you."

"Ben, no." She was losing him. Before he could leave, Bella stepped closer, pressing her hands against his chest. "I wanted to tell you the truth so many times, but I was afraid you'd never forgive me."

"You were right about that." He stepped away again, and her

hands dropped like ten-pound weights. "But that's the only thing you're right about. All that stuff about you belonging here? No way. You know where you belong? With your mother. From what I've seen of her—and what I know about you—you're just like her. A money-grubbing *Moody* through and through."

Her last name spewed from his lips like the curse word it was. "You're both pushy. Arrogant. Willing to do whatever it takes to get what you want. And there's no place for you here. Ever."

Bella sucked in air, nearly sinking to her knees. But she deserved this. Every word was true. She couldn't escape it.

Her legs wobbled, and a tear rolled down her cheek. "I'm so sorry I hurt you, Ben."

"I'll get over it. I always do." Then he spun and left her there.

And just as she'd been the first time she'd set foot in this town, Bella was all alone—her only family a woman who valued a business deal more than her daughter.

For longer than Bella wanted to admit, she stood there, mourning what might have been. But it had only ever been a fantasy.

The wind shifted, and she sighed. She couldn't change her reality. The only thing she could do was keep moving, forging her own destiny.

All by herself, always.

Bella strode back inside, grabbed her bags, got in her car, and pointed it toward home.

CHAPTER 12

Somehow, in a little more than twenty-four hours, Bella had to haul herself into work and face Mom again.

But for today, she'd see if she could beat yesterday's record for the number of Ben & Jerry's pints she could consume.

Snuggling under her blanket on the couch in her apartment, Bella dug her spoon into a carton of Half Baked. The *Shark Tank* judges argued from her television, vying for the chance to invest in a gadget that made unbuckling car seats easier. Their bickering resounded through the four-hundred-square-foot space. The place may be tiny, but it had always been her sanctuary.

Since returning from Walker Beach two nights ago, though, it just felt stark. Lonely.

There was a knock on her door, and whoever was there quickly became insistent. Bella was tempted to hide under her blanket—ridiculous because whoever was in the hallway couldn't see her.

A key clicked in the lock, and the handle turned.

Only one other person had a key to her place. "You'd better have dinner."

Jessica stepped through the doorway and held up a brown paper bag. "Antonio's okay?"

"The ultimate comfort food? Yes, definitely." Throwing off the blanket, Bella lumbered to her feet. "It'll go well with my third tub of ice cream."

Her best friend kicked the door shut behind her. "That's just wrong." She walked three steps and was in Bella's kitchen, where she set down the bag and pulled two containers from inside. "I got you the fettuccine. Hope that's OK. Or you can have my carbonara if you prefer."

Bella put the ice cream—spoon and all—back into the freezer then snagged two glasses from the cupboard. "Either one works." She pressed the first cup to the dispenser, and a shower of ice fell in.

Nose wrinkled, Jessica took in the full garbage can stuffed with takeout bags and cans of soda. "Have you left this place at all since you got back?"

Bella hadn't texted Jess that she was home until late last night just before falling asleep, so she'd been inside for forty-eight hours with no company other than TV. Jessica had cut hair all day but had promised to be over just as soon as her appointments were finished. And here she was—loyal with a capital L.

If only the same could be said of Mom.

Bella switched the dispenser to water and the liquid streamed into the glass, splashing over the edge onto her fingertips. "No." Full cups in hand, she turned, headed back to the couch, and placed the glasses onto two coasters on her coffee table.

Jess settled onto the couch next to Bella and slid Bella's fettuccine across the leather. She eyed an empty carton of Chunky Monkey on the table. "I'd ask how you're doing, but it seems obvious."

"Who, me? I'm fine." Bella popped the top on her to-go carton and inhaled the scent of butter and cheese—both of which would undoubtedly go straight to her hips. "I mean, my mom is a backstabber, and I lost a shot with the best man I've ever known, but you know." She picked up a fork and stabbed a piece of chicken nestled in the noodles.

"Right. You're fine."

"Totally fine." The tines of the fork pirouetted around the noodles, tying them up in a neat little knot before she brought them to her lips. Not even the divine taste of Antonio's could lift her spirits tonight. Of course, that wouldn't stop her from eating every bite.

"You ready to talk about it?"

"What's there to talk about?" Bella sipped her water, washing down the food that was overwhelming her taste buds with its richness. "I'm alone. I'm always going to be alone. That's the way it's destined to be. I mean, Mom's alone. And apparently, I'm just like her."

A flat, emotionless tone hovered in her voice, and she despised the pity party she was throwing herself. But the words smacked of truth, and what else was there to say, really?

"Bells, that doesn't have to be your life." Her food untouched, Jess leaned over to squeeze Bella's hand. "And you're not alone. I'm here."

Sighing, Bella patted Jess's fingers. "I know. And I'm grateful for you. But someday, an amazing man is going to sweep you off your feet and take you away from me."

"Even when that day finally arrives, you know I'll never leave you." Jess paused. "So. What happened in Walker Beach?"

"Mom showed up."

"Ugh."

"Ugh is right." Tomorrow she'd do everything she could to avoid Mom, which would be hard given their standing all-manager Monday meeting at one o'clock. Bella would have to sit on her hands the entire hour to keep herself from throwing something at Mom's head. But that wouldn't stop her from fantasizing about it. And yeah, she didn't care how immature that sounded.

Sighing, she told Jessica the whole rotten story. "All I wanted was a family to belong to. And I got blinded by that desire, willing to be just like Mom to beat her at her own game. But I turned it around, you know? Or so I thought. I even . . ."

"What?"

Shaking her head, she batted away a tear that had somehow snuck past her defenses. "When I was with Ben's family—when I was with *him*—it was like I'd always imagined it would be to have a family. Exactly what I'd been looking for, the reason I went to Walker Beach in the first place. It reminded me of the way I felt whenever I was with your family as a kid."

Jess smiled, fiddling with the lid of her carbonara. "Those were good times."

"The best." Bella shoved aside her half-eaten pasta. "For a moment, I thought maybe it was enough, you know? That I could be happy with pretending. But I realize that it's unlikely I'll find my dad's relatives, and that means I'll never belong to a real family. It'll always just be my mother and me—both of us alone and emotionally distant. What a life."

"I'm not sure I've ever seen you this melodramatic before." Jessica walked to the window and threw back the curtains. "You need to get out of this dark apartment. To remember that you're not alone. Not really."

The building next door blocked Bella's view from the fourth floor, a far cry from the beachfront vista courtesy of her little room at Ben's inn.

Her eyelids had turned gummy. But no. She didn't have a right to cry over this. She'd made her bed.

Striding to the window, Bella firmly closed the curtains again then flounced back to the freezer for her ice cream. "I'm not melodramatic. Just realistic." She leaned a hip against the counter and stuck a spoonful of frozen brownie and cookie dough into her mouth.

"Oh, we're back to lying to ourselves, are we?" Jess joined her in the kitchen, took a spoon from the silverware drawer, and dug into the carton in Bella's hand. "I hate seeing you like this. And I'm sorry about your dad's family and the way everything went down with Ben. But Bells"—she licked her spoon clean —"they're not your only chance at a real family. You know that I consider you a sister, right? My mom calls you her second daughter. You're *my* family."

Bella's lips trembled and not just from the cold spoon pressed against them. "I . . ."

"Believe me, I wouldn't hang out in just anyone's stinky apartment." Jess cracked a grin.

"Hey." She couldn't help the laugh that bubbled up in her chest. "Just because I haven't showered in a few days doesn't mean I stink."

"We'll have to agree to disagree." Jessica eased the spoon from Bella's hand and stuck it in the sink along with her own. "But I'm serious. Family isn't just about blood. It's about the bond you share. It's the people you choose to surround yourself with, to be there for. And I choose you."

Bella set the ice cream carton on the counter. "Oh, Jess." Sappiness wasn't her M.O., but she couldn't *not* follow that up with a hug. She wrapped her arms around her best friend. "I choose you too."

With a squeeze, Jess hugged and released Bella. Then she dug in the brown paper bag from Antonio's and emerged with a stack of napkins, which she held out to Bella. "Here. You look terrible."

Laughing, Bella took a napkin and swiped away a few stray tears. "Aren't you glad you came over? I'm such wonderful company."

"Are *you* glad I came over? Because I have one more thing to say, and you're not going to like it."

"You already called me stinky." Bella tossed the wet napkin at Jess. "What else could you have to say?"

But her friend didn't laugh. In fact, she nibbled at her bottom lip.

Great. Bella really *wasn't* going to like this. "Just spit it out."

"I know your mom has hurt you, but—"

"I'm gonna stop you right there. Because if you're about to say that I should forgive her, then you can save your breath. How can I? She betrayed me." Bella wasn't perfect by any means, but what had she done to deserve a mother like *that*?

"Come on, Bells."

"No, I can't. Just . . . sorry, Jess. I'm going to go take a bath so I don't stink anymore." Bella whirled on her heel.

"So you wanted Ben to forgive you, but you aren't willing to forgive your mom?"

Seriously? Bella jerked around to face Jess once again. "How can you even compare the two? I'm her daughter! She's supposed to love me more than anything or anyone. And she doesn't."

"I know she hasn't always acted like it. But maybe there's more to the story than you know." Jessica stared at the ground, her chin trembling, before she looked into Bella's eyes again. "And I'm not saying it'll be easy. But don't you see? If you don't forgive her, you'll never be free of this anger, this weight, this doubting that you belong. It's a chain around your neck, weighing you down. And it's killing you."

Bella slumped against the counter, sliding down along the cabinets until her butt hit the floor. Her breath rattled in and out, noisy and erratic.

And then Jess was beside her, leaning her head on Bella's shoulder. "I know you like being in control, but you've been letting bitterness control you instead. So don't do it for your mom. Do it for you. Because Bells, I don't think that you can ever be free until you let it go."

"I don't know how to."

"I'm no expert. But maybe just try talking to your mom. Tell her how you feel. Open the lines of communication." A squeeze to her hand. "And whatever her response is, you can't let it change how you see yourself. Your worth, your sense of belonging, can't be found in your mom. You are a beautiful creation, loved by God, loved by me, and loved by so many others. If your mom doesn't see that, then she's a fool."

Bella's heart pounded, leaping at the idea of freedom and colliding with the idea of talking with her mom.

But maybe Jessica was right. Maybe, regardless of what happened with Mom, whatever could have been with Ben, Bella could find a place to belong. In fact, perhaps she already had one.

She just needed to reach out and embrace it as her own.

CHAPTER 13

*H*e should have started working on the inn's staircase by now.

But what was the point?

From Ben's spot in the bed of his truck, he blinked at the ocean stretching out in front of him. Early-morning surfers stood on boards, riding the waves and taking whatever life threw their way without wiping out.

Apparently, Ben was not so talented.

After attempting to get stuff done around the inn the day after Bella left—and failing miserably—he'd hopped into his truck and started driving. When he couldn't keep his eyes open any longer, he'd pulled over onto some random beach a few hours north of town. Yesterday, he'd mostly lazed around here then walked to the nearest town and grabbed a pizza before returning to his truck and sleeping again on the beach.

From the phone next to him, music blared. A Tim McGraw song ended, and a new song popped on—Alan Jackson singing about a betrayal he hadn't seen coming.

Join the club, Alan.

Huffing out a harsh breath in between bites of cold pizza—breakfast of champions—Ben silenced the music, the quiet leaving him once again with his thoughts.

Thoughts he did not want.

About a gorgeous woman with tan skin and blond-streaked brown hair and the deepest chocolate eyes.

Eyes he should have known not to trust. Numerous people had warned him. But had Ben listened? Nope. He'd fallen for the same old tricks, the same old lies.

And at the end of the day, he was still going to lose his inn, probably to the mother of the woman who had betrayed him.

So why work against the inevitable? Maybe it was time to give in to the failure.

Still, he couldn't run away forever. It was time to go home. Ben swung his legs off the truck bed and groaned at the ache pounding in his temple. Only a few hours of sleep in two consecutive nights would do that to a guy.

He climbed back into the cab of the truck, started it, and headed south. After a few hours and a gallon of gas station coffee, he took the exit to Walker Beach and pulled into the inn's parking lot.

Which was full.

He rubbed his eyes, but the assortment of cars and trucks remained. And he recognized every one of them. As he got out of his vehicle, the familiar white noise of a concrete mixer and muted shouts from behind the inn met his ears.

What the . . .

He jogged to the courtyard gate and pulled up at the sight in front of him. A team of guys in hardhats poured concrete. Scanning the group, Ben identified cousins and uncles. And there was Dad, giving directions, leading the pack.

They'd already torn out the broken wooden staircase and made nice headway on pouring the concrete foundation where the bottom step would rest. Another team of men measured and cut wooden boards on the other side of the yard, while still others transferred stone pavers from the back of a truck into a stack near the wall.

From the look of things, they wouldn't be able to finish the stairs completely because the concrete would take three days or so to cure. Still, with this many people working, they'd easily knock out the majority of the building today.

But the question remained—why were they fixing his inn in the first place?

Ben moved past a pile of hardhats and work gloves toward his father. Talking loudly over the various compressors and other whirring tools, Dad slapped Uncle Lucas on the back. He turned at Ben's approach. "Hey, son. I wondered when we'd finally see you."

"Didn't know I'd be seeing you at all. What are you doing here?"

"That's a question for your sister. She's upstairs." Dad paused. "When you're done talking with her, we could use some help getting the staircase going."

With a nod, Ben headed through the outside door that led into the kitchen. There he found a mostly demolished stack of pancakes and a side platter of breakfast meats. And in the middle of the table, the crowning glory—an entire pan of what looked like Grandma's famous cake batter blondies. A stack of freshly washed plates and cups sat in the drying rack to the right of the sink.

A thump sounded overhead, and Ben strode through the hallway and up the stairs. Chest hitching, he paused before entering the lobby, which he hadn't set foot in since Bella had left on Thursday.

A laugh drifted down the staircase. When he reached the top stair and turned, his jaw slackened. The upper floor of his inn was overrun with females—aunts and cousins of all ages—

scrubbing walls, tearing down the gold wallpaper border ringing the ceiling, and covering the furniture with plastic. A small group appeared to be well into applying a vivid blue color to the walls of the south hallway, which led to a handful of guest rooms.

Ben's eyes roamed until he located his mom and sister deep in conversation by the fireplace. Ashley examined a document in her hands.

He cleared his throat as he approached them. "Uh, what's going on here?"

Ashley turned, her eyes bright. "Ben! I was starting to worry about you. You didn't answer any of my messages for the last few days."

He had seen her calls and texts but hadn't wanted to talk. "I'm fine. Just went out of town for a bit." Running a hand through his hair, he frowned. "You didn't answer my question."

Mom, dressed in a ratty T-shirt and leggings, her eyes soft, pressed a hand to his cheek. "Aw, honey, you look so tired. I'm sorry we didn't come before now."

"Why *did* you come now? What are you guys doing?"

"I'll let you two talk." Mom moved to help Aunt Kiki tape a wall.

He turned back to Ashley. "I'll ask again. Why is the entire Baker clan taking over my inn?"

She held up the papers. "I stopped by yesterday and couldn't find you. But I did find this."

He snatched it, his eyes raking over the words *Iridescent Inn Business Plan*. Bella must have printed a copy when she'd created it a few weeks ago and left it lying around. Shoving it into Ashley's hands, he planted his feet and crossed his arms. "I don't want anything to do with that."

Ashley's eyes grew sad. She tilted her head. "I'm sorry about Bella. I really liked you guys together."

Why did he bother ever trying to have secrets in this stupid little town? "I did too until I found out she was a lying . . ." He held back a not-so-nice name. "That's irrelevant. What *is* relevant is why you're here."

His sister had the audacity to look amused. "Actually, it's kind of relevant because Bella *is* the reason we're here."

"I don't follow."

"She stopped by my apartment to say goodbye Thursday night. Told me everything." Ashley set the business plan on the coffee table. "I have to admit, for a moment I wanted to slap her."

"As if you would ever slap anyone."

"But I wanted to." Ashley frowned. "I think she's truly sorry, and she cares about you, Ben."

"I don't—"

"No, listen." Ashley rarely raised her voice. When she did, people tended to listen.

Ben grunted for her to go on.

"She told me that the inn was struggling but that you refused to ask for help out of some misguided sense that you had to do it on your own."

He could picture Bella saying those words, a mixture of love and determination in them. A small smile snuck onto his lips.

But no. Bella Moody didn't know how to love.

Only deceive.

His molars ground together. "So you're all here out of pity?"

"No, dummy. We're here because we care about you. Oh, and Evan sends his regrets. He's working for Chrissy again or he'd be here."

"Seems like there's plenty of help anyway."

"Yeah, I think we've had about twenty or thirty in and out. Some came right at six and worked for a bit but had to leave already. Grandma was here earlier to make breakfast for everyone. She needed to go home to rest but said she'll be back with dinner." Ashley fiddled with a piece of her long hair, which was pulled back into a ponytail. "I hope you're not upset that we just took over in here. It needed a makeover, and you know how women like a good reno project."

"I didn't have a clue what to do, so I'm OK with whatever you chose."

"Really?" Ashley frowned. "Your business plan had some good guidance. We're improvising a bit but mostly sticking to that. And we won't finish it today, but we're making progress."

He didn't remember anything about improving the lobby in the plan Bella had given him, but maybe he'd just been so focused on the outer repairs to notice. "Thanks, sis. I owe you." Slinging an arm around her shoulders, he squeezed. "I'd better go pull my weight outside."

"I'll hold down the fort in here."

"I know you will." He plunged down the stairs, changed into some work-appropriate clothing, and headed outside. Ben approached Dad as he slid on a pair of gloves. "Put me to work."

For hours, he worked alongside his dad, who passed tools and boards up the ladder so Ben could install the new treads and risers to the staircase where their ladder didn't interfere with the hardening concrete pad. They only took a break for a quick lunch of sandwiches and potato salad that his cousins Shannon and Lia had made.

As evening approached, the sun almost at the spot where the beach met the sea, Ben sat sipping lemonade on the deck. Every muscle in his body ached, but his inn looked like a million bucks. It sparkled and shone even more than the glittering ocean taking up the expanse of his view.

Yet his pride had taken a beating today. He'd talked to so many relatives, answering the same questions over and over again. About what the future of the inn looked like. About his plans. And about Bella.

His grandma had presented him with a blondie, cocking her

head and asking where his pretty little girlfriend was. *"She's spunky. I like her."*

He hadn't had the heart to tell everyone the truth, probably more to protect himself than her reputation. If people knew he'd been an idiot twice over, there'd be no living that down. It would be bad enough when they found out he would probably have to sell the inn they'd put their blood and sweat into.

At least all the improvements would fetch a nice price for the place. Maybe he could find a buyer who was just as committed to keeping Moody Development out.

The door slid open behind him, unleashing the chatter of the few family members who'd stuck it out this long and were enjoying dessert inside. Glancing up, Ben spied his father, who settled into the Adirondack chair beside him, water bottle in hand.

"Thanks for coming today." Ben cringed at the way his voice croaked.

"I'll always come when one of my kids needs me." Dad popped the top of his water. "Of course, it helps if they ask."

The lingering taste of disgrace flared on Ben's tongue. Or maybe it was just the lemonade. He shook his head. "I couldn't."

"And why not?"

"Because . . ."

Dad took a sip and wiped his mouth with the back of his beefy hand. Waited for Ben to gather his thoughts.

Ben blew out a breath. "I wanted to be like you. Like Grandpa. Like all my aunts and uncles." His throat closed. "Successful. But look at me. I've ruined the legacy I've been handed. It's unlikely I'll recover from this slump, Dad."

Ben leaned forward, elbows on knees, and rubbed his eyes. The scent of sawdust still hung in the air.

"Son, I don't say it enough, but I'm proud of you."

Straightening, he turned to stare at Dad. "Proud? Why? Didn't you hear me? I'm going to lose the inn." He stood and gripped the railing. "Pretty sure I'm not someone you should be proud of."

Chair legs scratched against the deck as his dad ambled to his feet, his strong and steady presence wrapping around Ben as he approached.

For a moment, everything was still.

"I remember feeling the same way when I lost my first business."

"I'm sorry, what?" Ben's gaze shot toward his father.

Dad chuckled as he tossed back the rest of his water then set the empty bottle on the ground. "I was twenty-two, married for about a year, and we'd just found out your mom was pregnant with you." His fingers splayed on his jaw, stroking as he looked up at the first stars starting to populate the sky. "When I was nineteen, I'd started a painting business. Hired a few guys, built a solid list of clientele in Walker Beach and just beyond. But suffice it to say I made some poor investments, some bad choices, and I trusted the wrong people."

Sounded familiar.

His father looked at him again. "The point is, I had to declare bankruptcy and get a job working as an entry-level clerk in the hardware store for Chrissy Price's father. And I had a wife, a son on the way. To say I was ashamed is an understatement. Thought I'd failed the Baker name, set a horrible example for all my younger siblings who were looking up to me."

"So what happened?"

"My dad took me aside and explained real success."

Had Grandpa been disappointed in Dad for his failures? "Yeah, I already know that part. Real success means owning businesses, stepping up to be leaders in the community."

"No, Ben." Dad turned and gripped his son's shoulder. "He told me that success isn't about what you do. It's about who you are. Whether you stand up for what's right. Whether you fight for things that matter. Leading isn't about owning a business, son. It's about doing what's right and being there for the people you love. It's about admitting when you're wrong and doing better the next time. About not quitting. About being humble enough to ask for help when you need it."

Instead of the slap Ben had expected, the words filtered over him, through him, smoothing the rough edges inside. He finally felt like he could breathe again. "So, if I lose the inn . . ."

"I'll still be just as proud of you as I always am."

"But I'd be losing Grandpa's legacy. How could you be proud of that?"

"If your grandfather were here, I'm positive he would tell you that his legacy was never in a building. It was in his family. *You* are his legacy, Ben—not this inn."

Wow. The relief was the prick in the ballooning shame that had been sitting in Ben's chest, growing and pushing outward till it ached. "Thanks, Dad."

"And Ben?"

"Yeah?"

"I may have been wrong before. When I told you to focus on saving the inn instead of love." He scratched behind his ear. "I admit I just didn't want to see you get hurt again. But I should have supported you, respected you enough to butt out and let you make your own choice."

Ben made a fist and bumped it lightly against the railing. "Nah, you were right on that count, Dad. I put my faith in the wrong person, just like you told me not to."

"I don't know what she did, but people make mistakes some-times. A lot of times, actually. But as you're learning, it's not our mistakes that define us. It's what we do with them."

And what had Bella done?

Left, that's what.

But he couldn't let *her* actions dictate his. Not anymore. Thanks to his family—the people who really loved him—he'd made huge strides toward reopening the inn. Maybe it wouldn't be enough.

Or maybe, just maybe, it would.

"Thanks, Dad." Ben pulled his dad into a man hug, thumping his back. "Now, if you'll excuse me, I have an inn to save."

CHAPTER 14

*I*f this didn't work, he wasn't sure what he'd do.

As soon as the maintenance man unlocked the front doors of City Hall on Monday morning, Ben barged through, marching straight for Evan's office.

The answer to at least his immediate problems had come to him at midnight. He'd forgotten about the grant. It had been too late to text his friend, so here he was eight hours later to find out if Evan could grease some wheels and make things happen before Ben lost his chance.

City Hall was mostly empty at this hour, the smell of lemony floor wax fresh in the air. Maybe he should have waited until more workers arrived. What time did Evan get in, anyway?

Not that it mattered. He'd wait all day if he had to.

When he reached the office with the placard outside proclaiming it the community development office, Ben knocked. No one answered, so he turned and leaned back, one foot propped against the wall.

"Can I help you?" A pregnant red-headed woman who looked to be in her late thirties stood there with a ring of keys in one hand and a Java's Village Bean coffee in the other.

He'd met Evan's boss once before but couldn't quite remember her name. Donna? Diana?

"Yeah, hi. I was stopping by to see Evan Walsh. I'm Ben Baker."

"I remember you. Denise Goyer." The woman unlocked the door and pushed, angling the doorstopper at the bottom down to prop it open. "And I'm sorry. I got a text from Evan this morning. He's planning to be out all week." She flicked the lights on and moved inside the cramped office, setting her purse and coffee on one of the three desks.

"Oh, I didn't know that. I hope everything's OK."

Denise lowered herself into her chair, grunting slightly. "I understand that Chrissy Price doesn't have long. He wanted to be there with her when . . ." She sighed as she fired up her computer.

"Man, I didn't realize." And here he was worried about his inn. He'd have to text Evan to see if there were anything he could do.

"But I'm happy to help you if I can." Placing one hand on her rounded stomach, Denise took a sip from her coffee.

"That would be great." Ben glanced around for a chair and finally settled on stealing Evan's from behind his desk. He wheeled it over and plopped down. "Evan was looking into some grants for my inn. He said you guys secure them through a bunch of different sources and give them to local businesses that need help."

"We do." The computer screen popped on, and Denise turned to type in her credentials. "And he mentioned it to me several weeks ago. I believe he was still waiting to hear about a substantial grant that would be distributed in chunks to several businesses around town."

"Right." Ben fidgeted in his seat. "Would you mind checking on the status of that?"

Denise's lips tightened with a forced smile. She probably had a million other things to do on a Monday morning.

But Ben had to fight. After all the work his family had put into helping him, how could he not? Because for the first time, instead of seeing the inn as a burden, he'd embraced it as the gift it was—a piece of his family history, a home, a beacon of stability in a life filled with uncertainty.

The community development officer clicked around on the computer for a minute or two before squinting at the screen. "Oh." She sat back in her seat. "It appears the grant came through on Friday after Evan and I had left for the day."

"Really?"

"Yes." She flashed a real smile this time. "And according to Evan's dispersal plan, you're set to receive a fourth of it." Denise named the amount he'd receive.

His blood pumped faster. "Wow." It was more than Evan had anticipated.

Yeah, Ben would still need to work hard to attract new customers, but for the moment, his inn was saved. He did some quick calculations in his head, figuring that he'd be able to pay back the bank as well as his mortgage and other expenses for at least six months.

"Thank you so much."

"Happy to help. I hope you can put it to good use." Denise did some more clicking, and a printer in the corner whirred to life. "We should be able to cut you a check by Friday."

"Fantastic."

"Here." She snagged a paper off the printer and handed it to him. "All the details. And feel free to call me if you have any questions."

With thanks, he pumped her hand and headed home in his truck. The sun streaked across the August sky, nearly blinding him with its brilliance. Ben flipped down his visor as he drove.

Things had really turned around. From flat-out failure to success.

But success had come even before this moment. Because like Dad had said last night, it wasn't about actually saving the inn, though Ben was grateful he had a shot. Really, it was about keeping on, not giving up. About fighting and accepting help.

He pulled into the empty parking lot of the inn and turned off his truck. Climbing out, he stared at the building he called home. Later this week, he'd finish the staircase. Today, maybe he could work on getting new flooring into one of the upstairs guest rooms.

The Iridescent Inn was almost ready for guests again.

His fingers itched to pull his phone from his pocket and call Bella, tell her the good news.

Argh. Would he never be free of this hold she had over him? Even more than it had with Elena, his heart ached over the loss of her. Of what they'd had—if any of it had been real in the first place.

And he couldn't trust that was the case.

As he strode inside, his dad's words drifted back to him: *"I don't know what she did, but people make mistakes sometimes. A lot of times, actually. But as you're learning, it's not our mistakes that define us. It's what we do with them."*

No. She'd chosen her path, and it didn't include Ben.

He headed to his office to drop off the paper Denise had given him. When Ben opened the door, the room gave off a musty odor. Made sense. He couldn't remember the last time he'd been in here.

Stepping inside, he set the paper on his desk. There, on his keyboard, a document with a bright yellow sticky note caught his eye. Ben picked it up and scanned the words written there. *If you haven't read this in-depth yet, you need to. Love, Ashley*

What was his sister up to now? He peeled off the note and stared at the same document she'd been carrying around yesterday—the business plan Bella had worked up weeks ago.

Ben fell into his chair, staring at the document. He considered tossing it into the trash.

But wait. Underneath *Iridescent Inn Business Plan*, it said, *Updated August 6.*

That was last Thursday. The day she'd left.

What had she added since he'd last seen it?

Ben flipped to the first page. The mission statement, vision statement, all the stuff he and Bella had already hashed out were there. The following pages detailed the preliminary plan they'd outlined.

But then . . . whoa. There had to be at least fifteen, maybe twenty more pages here.

Laying out specific ways he could cut expenses.

Detailed low-cost marketing efforts.

Ways to use assets he already had.

Cost-effective renovations he could make to increase the quality of stay for guests without breaking his bank.

Ben raised his eyebrows. By giving him this, Bella had guaranteed he'd have the ammunition to bounce back and refuse her mother's offer once and for all.

And it also meant that if Bella had been telling the truth, she was sacrificing the one thing she'd longed for—to know who her dad had been, to find his family.

Maybe she had made a mistake in lying to him. But this business plan proved that not all of it had been a lie.

That indefinable thing between them had been real. Which meant he hadn't been a fool after all. Hadn't been duped twice. Not really.

Because deep down, he knew exactly who Bella Moody was.

And he wasn't ready to let her go.

So far, she'd kept herself focused on the meeting.

Mostly.

It probably helped that one of Moody Development's vice presidents, Lincoln Chase—not Mom—was conducting the meeting in the company's conference room. Mom sat to his right, as poised as ever, hands folded in front of her on the ten-person modern white table.

Anytime Mom looked at her Bella glanced away, deflecting the burning coal in her dark eyes. And if she could just keep her gaze on the PowerPoint slides behind Lincoln and her mother's heads for a few more minutes, she wouldn't have to worry about shooting eye darts back at Mom while surrounded by her fellow company executives.

"Does anyone have any questions?" Lincoln, a forty-something blond with impeccable style, adjusted his thick-rimmed glasses.

"Not a question, but I did want to update everyone on something."

All heads—even Bella's—turned toward Mom.

The white ruffles trailing down the front of her Burberry blouse fluttered as the air conditioner kicked on from the vent above her. "We've decided to move on from the Walker Beach proposal. The last property holdout could not be convinced to sell." She arched a perfectly plucked eyebrow at Bella. "I want to be honest with you. This puts the company in a bit of a precarious position."

Bella's cheeks burned as her coworkers followed Mom's gaze. Most of the team knew she'd been out for several weeks trying to secure Ben's property. And now they knew she'd failed.

She bit the inside of her cheek to keep from saying something she'd regret.

How could Jess ask Bella to forgive a woman who would blame her own daughter for the company's impending bankruptcy—and in front of everyone, no less? How could *Bella* have thought for a second that forgiveness might be possible?

It was too much to ask.

Mom cleared her throat. "Because of this failure, we are going to be forced to move quickly on some other projects we had meant for the winter pipeline."

The other managers began to murmur, but Mom cut them off with the wave of her hand. "I'm going to email out details by the end of business today about what I need from each of you to make this a success."

Though her features were tight, she smiled, searching the faces of each manager—save Bella—before speaking again. "All of you are essential members of the team, and I know that together we can make Moody Development stronger than it's ever been."

Her mother sure could lay on the charm when she wanted to. And judging by the looks on the other executives' faces, they believed her.

"I think we're all done here for today unless anyone has anything to add." When no one spoke up, she gathered the papers in front of her, shutting them in a folder. "You're dismissed. Bella, could we please speak in my office?"

Bella rubbed the goosebumps that popped along her arms. "Of course." How she managed to keep the words steady, she didn't know. She stood, lightheaded, but ignored the white spots in her vision as she followed Mom.

Her mother breezed into her corner office, which overlooked a park adjacent to the business complex in a small suburb just twenty miles outside of downtown Los Angeles. Then she slid into the white midback office chair behind the desk. "Close the door behind you."

Bella did so then approached Mom's desk. Continuing to stand, she crossed her arms. "Yes?"

"I want to talk about what happened on Thursday."

How could Mom sound so . . . composed? Bella's body tensed as she wrestled with the rage and hurt threatening to leap out of her. For a moment her gaze tripped back to the park, to a pair of trees planted too close to each other. The roots had started coming up through the ground.

There wasn't enough space, weren't enough nutrients, for both, and one had clearly started to yield to the other. Even from several yards away, Bella could see how it listed to one side, its leaves scarcer, its bark discolored.

Averting her eyes, she choked out a reply. "OK."

Mom propped her head against one hand, her fingertips drumming along her cheekbone. "Don't you feel you have something to say to me?"

"I have a lot of things to say. But I'm trying not to say them, as they won't do any good."

"I see." Her mother picked up a photo frame from the front of her desk—the one Bella knew contained a picture of the two of them, hugging and happy. Some relic from her childhood. Ghosts from their past.

Mom lightly stroked the edge of the black frame with her thumb. "I suppose I shouldn't be surprised. You've shown where your loyalty lies."

"My loy—" Bella inhaled through her nose. Normally, she didn't mind verbal sparring.

But normally, she didn't have so much at stake.

She tried again. "Mom, I'm sorry that the company is moving toward bankruptcy. I really am. But—"

"No, Bella, it's clear you don't care what becomes of this company. You've chosen a side, and it isn't with me."

"Why would I choose a woman who has *never* chosen me?"

Oops.

The look on Mom's face—eyes dull, mouth slack, eyebrows knit together—showed everything. Bella's words had shocked her mother as much as they'd surprised Bella.

"Never chosen you? What is that supposed to mean?"

She really wanted to know? Fine. Bella yanked back the

chair on the opposite side of the desk and plopped down. "Ever since you went back to school, you have chosen everything else before me."

"I went back to school *for* you. So you'd have a better life than I did." Mom dropped the picture back on the desk as if it had burned her palm.

"How was it better for you to be gone all the time?" Bella's arms wrapped around her stomach. "Before, we were poor, sure, but we were happy."

"I wasn't."

"Well, I was."

"That wouldn't have lasted. Believe me." Something distant in Mom's eyes signaled a life, a past, that Bella knew nothing about.

A prick of sympathy wound through her. "Maybe not." She bit her lip. "But Mom, even if your initial motivation was me, it didn't stay that way. In trying to give me the best life, you missed so much of my childhood. And you're missing out on my adulthood because your company is more important than me."

Do not cry, do not cry, do not cry.

Mom sat staring at her for several long moments. The sunlight coming in through the glass behind Mom's head revealed smudges on the floor-to-ceiling window. "I'm sorry you believe that, though I can see why you do." Rubbing her forehead, she winced. "And I'll admit, there is a certain addiction that can develop when you finally feel powerful and in control for the first time."

"When have you ever *not* been in control?"

"How about the time I was left alone and pregnant at the age of nineteen?"

Right. Bella slumped in the chair. "That must have been rough. But surely Daniel—Dad—wouldn't have left you if he'd had a choice. I mean, he died. You can't blame him for that."

Mom sighed. "I lied, Bella."

Why should she be surprised? "About what?"

"He didn't die. At least, that I know of." The words sliced through the room. "As you know, we were never married. What you don't know is that he was nothing more than a weekend fling. My girlfriends and I were on spring break and driving up the coast. We stopped in Walker Beach, and I met Daniel there."

Bella leaned forward. Finally. She was finally going to learn about her father.

"He took me out for steak and shrimp then shopping for fancy art at the gallery in town. I convinced my friends to stay one extra night so I could be with him. It all felt so exciting for a poor college student to meet a handsome man with money to burn." Mom's voice softened with the memories. "He was more than that, though. He was a good sort of man. But he didn't want to tell me his last name or where he lived, which makes me think . . ."

Oh. What had started as a sweet story turned bitter. But however distasteful, she had to know the rest. "Was he seeing someone else?"

Shrugging, Mom fiddled with one of her manicured nails. "Or married. He was several years older than me. Thirty-two, I think."

"Did you ever see him again?"

Mom shook her head. "I found out I was pregnant six weeks later. Went to Walker Beach to try to track him down but no one had ever heard of him except for this kind teacher who worked weekends at the inn where I'd stayed."

"Mary Robinson?"

"I don't know. Maybe. She remembered seeing Daniel and me together but had never seen him before that weekend. She even checked the hotel records for me, but he must have stayed under an assumed name. And with only a first name to go on, no one else I asked around town could tell me anything."

The truth burned away Bella's last kindling of hope. "I don't understand why you lied to me about him dying. And why not tell me all of this long before now?"

"You really don't get it? I'm ashamed, Bella." Turning, Mom gazed out the window. "Do you realize how many women I knew who got pregnant at fifteen, sixteen? There was even one girl who had a baby when she was twelve. I may have grown up in a trailer park, but I stayed away from boys, studied hard in school, got into college, was working my way through. Then in one night, I threw all of that away."

"Sorry I ruined your life so much."

Mom whipped her chair around so fast the wheels squeaked on the polished floor. "You didn't." An emotion flashed in her eyes, something almost foreign—something that looked like fierce protectiveness. Maybe even love.

Bella hadn't glimpsed a look like that on Mom's face in a really long time.

She swallowed hard. "I didn't?"

"You changed the trajectory of my life, but you didn't ruin it. In fact, you gave me a reason to work harder than I ever had." Sighing, Mom tapped the edge of the desk. "Though I can admit now that perhaps you're right—I started off doing it for you, but along the way, it became about me. About proving to myself that I could turn things around, become someone important, someone that a man like Daniel wouldn't easily forget."

Oh, Mom. Bella itched to round the desk and hug her mother, but she stayed in her chair. "Is that why you fought so hard to build the resort in Walker Beach?"

"I suppose so. Maybe deep down I imagined him seeing it and feeling some sort of regret. How utterly ridiculous."

"Not so ridiculous. I certainly understand it."

"But it's no excuse for how I've made you feel." Mom frowned. "I . . . I'm sorry, Bella."

"I forgive you, Mom." The words that had seemed so impossible minutes ago now felt right and true.

"Well." Mom's jaw tensed, and she swerved her chair toward the computer. "I have a lot of work to do. You can leave the door open on the way out."

That was all the reply she was going to get? No hug? No warm words about doing better in the future?

She supposed she shouldn't have expected anything more from her mother.

"Don't do it for your mom. Do it for you. Because, Bells, I don't think that you can ever be free until you let it go." Jessica's words from last night tossed peace over her shoulders like a warm blanket.

The tightening in Bella's chest lessened, and her breathing normalized.

Oh.

So that's what freedom felt like.

Jess had been right. And, yeah, maybe Bella's offer of forgiveness hadn't outwardly affected Mom.

But it was affecting Bella.

Mom's reaction and all that she'd revealed about Bella's father was a good reminder of the other thing Jessica had said— that family was who she chose. She didn't have to wait around for some discovery. She didn't have to wait around for an embrace from her mom that might never come.

She could keep living her life, choosing who to love and who to call her own.

And there was freedom in that.

"OK." Bella stood and strode toward the door. "I'll see you later."

"Bella."

Her steps hitched. She swung her gaze back to her mom. "Yes?"

"Thank you. For your honesty." Mom's whole body remained stiff, but Bella could swear she saw her upper lip tremble. "And . . . for your forgiveness."

A smile stretched across Bella's lips. "I love you, Mom."

"Yes, yes, I love you too. Now get back to work."

"Yes, ma'am." Shaking her head, Bella headed toward her office, crossing through the reception area on her way back.

"Bella." The receptionist, Toni, flagged her down. "Your two o'clock is in your office."

She couldn't remember any appointments on the books, but Bella didn't want Toni to know that. "Thanks, Toni."

The receptionist popped her gum and leaned forward, a saucy smile on her face. "And girl, he is fine." She drew out the last word.

Bella's limbs tingled. It wasn't . . . no. Ben wasn't the only handsome man on the planet.

Most handsome? Yes. But not the only one.

"Noted." Smoothing out the wrinkles in her purple blouse, Bella walked down the hallway, heels clicking on the floor as she rounded the corner to her office.

She peeked in—and her heart nearly stopped.

There was Ben, sitting in her chair, feet propped up on her desk, hands folded over his stomach, eyes closed as if he didn't have a care in the world.

Why was he here? And why did he have to look so fiiiiiiiiine, as Toni had said? His unshaven jaw showed days of growth, but despite her normal preference for a clean face, the stubble heightened his appeal.

"Ben?"

He sat upright so quickly that he nearly fell out of the chair. Then he flashed her a sheepish grin. "Hey."

"What are you doing here?"

The maroon T-shirt he wore brought out the deep brown flecks of his eyes in a way that weakened her knees. "I came to tell you what an idiot I am."

She slumped against the doorframe. "What?"

Standing, he maneuvered around the desk and came toward

her. He reached for her hand, pulled her out of the doorway, and shut the door. Then he turned toward her. "I found the business plan you left for me."

"Oh." She'd wondered if he would.

"It made me realize that I was wrong." He smoothed the skin on the back of her hand with his thumb, sending delicious tingles up her spine. "I'm sorry I sent you away."

"You had every right to."

"Maybe." He cocked his head. "But it was all about wounded pride for me. I couldn't believe I'd fallen for another woman who had lied to me. But you're not the same as Elena, as much as I tried to make you out to be."

"Ben, I was worse." She bit her lip. "But I *am* sorry. I truly never wanted to hurt you. And then, as things got real between us, I didn't want to lose you. But I did anyway."

"I'm sorry for not having more faith in you. I should have believed in you, believed in us. Believed what I knew was true."

"And what's that?"

"Bella, I don't need to see your birth certificate. I know who you are." He paused. "Who you really are."

Her lips trembled. "Ben."

"And I know your last name is Moody, but you don't belong here at Moody Development."

"I don't?"

He shook his head, slid his arms around her waist. "You belong at the Iridescent Inn. With me."

Fireworks burst in her chest. It was too much. Forgiving her mom had freed Bella. But being forgiven imparted a joy she didn't deserve. "I like the sound of that." She studied this man who had given her so much. Hope ringed his eyes, and she couldn't help but tease him. "Does that mean you're offering me a job?"

"Would you take it if I did?"

"Maybe." She cocked her head. "Is the pay any good?"

"Terrible."

"Tempting. What about paid time off?"

"Not so much."

"Hmmm. And what kind of benefits package do you offer?"

"Now *that* is one of our strongest selling points. It includes lots of hours working with the handsome owner of the inn. And, when appropriate, lots of kissing." His mouth slid into a wicked grin. "I'm happy to give you a sample of these amazing benefits if you'd like."

"I don't think I'd be able to make my decision without one."

Ben ran his finger along the side of her face, tucking her hair behind her ear. His thumb settled under her cheekbone, and his other hand pulled her flush against him. Then he bent toward her, pressing his lips to hers.

His kiss tasted of promise and sunshine and . . . life. Sweet, sweet life.

She pulled away, lips tingling. "To be honest, yours seems quite competitive with other offers I've received."

"Other offers?" He growled the words, tightened his hold.

"Naturally." Bella laughed and reached up to stroke his cheek, the stubble soft beneath her fingertips, much to her surprise. "How are you going to make your offer stand out above the rest?"

"What if I threw my heart into the mix?" His eyes caught hers, and she nearly melted at the intensity shining there.

Bella settled her arms around his neck. "Now we're getting somewhere."

"Does that mean you'll come back with me? Help me whip the inn into shape?"

"Yes, but it means more than that. It means I choose you, Ben."

His fingers skimmed her chin. "I choose you too, Bella. Your past, your present, your future—no matter your last name." Ben kissed her again. "I choose all of you. Always."

EPILOGUE

*W*hoever said "many hands make light work" knew what they were talking about.

Massaging his left shoulder, Ben looked out over the inn's courtyard from the deck above. His sister, Shannon, and Bella scurried back and forth from the kitchen to the various outdoor spaces, ensuring that everything was all set for the Iridescent Inn's first luau.

While Ben had done some of the heavy lifting—literally—the women were the ones who had made the place shine, with tiki torches lining the path, first from the parking lot to the gate then down to the inn's private beach. Tables with fancy pineapple centerpieces were scattered throughout the courtyard, and the smell of roasted pig twined its way up from the beach.

Nikki Harding and her band did a mic test near the courtyard fountain, the sound of her ukulele echoing through the rented sound system.

The whole thing had been Bella's brilliant idea, and Ashley had been only too thrilled to use her event planning expertise to make tonight a reality despite the three-and-a-half short weeks they'd had to pull it together. According to Ash, they'd already sold enough tickets to put Ben in the black for the rest of the year—and that didn't even include all the out-of-town guests coming in for the long weekend who planned to attend the Walker Beach Labor Day picnic tomorrow.

For the first time since Ben had inherited the inn, it was full.

Evan came up beside him and leaned on the railing. "Everything looks great, man."

"Thanks. And thanks for giving up your Friday night to be here."

"Where else would I be?" His friend's voice betrayed his grief. A few days after Ben had made things right with Bella, Chrissy Price had slipped into a coma and passed away not long after. It had only been three weeks, and the wound was still fresh for Evan. For everyone in town, really.

"How are you doing, dude?"

Evan fixed his gaze on the horizon. Though the sky featured a slightly hazy film, the sun still brightened the beach and would for another hour and a half. "It's hard. She was more than a mentor to me. She was one of my best friends."

His breath shuddered out. He coughed. "Anyway, I'm glad you're doing this luau. I know it's benefitting you, but it's also a great thing for the city. Between you and me, the economy has taken a hit since the earthquake. There just aren't as many visitors as there were before, and local businesses are suffering for it. I'm doing my best to hand out grants, but only so many exist." He frowned. "There's one opportunity I'm pursuing, but . . . I don't know. It almost feels like an affront to Chrissy's memory, you know?"

"How's that?"

"A regional hardware store may be interested in opening a location here."

"Oh." Made sense why that would be hard for Evan. "Is

Chrissy's store closing, then? I assumed she left it to a family member."

Then again, Chrissy didn't have any family in town. Her mother hadn't even held her memorial service in Walker Beach, so the community had chosen to hold its own vigil at the local church where Ben's cousin, Spencer, pastored.

"She left the store to her niece, Madison. Guess she used to live here with Chrissy. Supposedly, she's in grad school in LA, but she hasn't contacted anyone in town to inform us of her plans for the store yet." Evan straightened, shoved his hands in the pocket of his jeans. "Chrissy figured Madison would just sell it, so this regional hardware store opportunity shouldn't inter-fere—except maybe to diminish the value of Chrissy's store."

"I can see why it's a hard call."

"Yeah. I'll hold off for a bit just to make sure, but it may be too good of an opportunity for Walker Beach to pass up. It would bring more jobs and such to town."

"Sounds like a good thing."

"Are you gentlemen just going to stand there all night?"

Ben turned to find a smirking Bella standing at the top of the stairs, hands on her hips. She looked amazing—and cold—in a strappy little dress with blue Hawaiian flowers.

Intelligent, resourceful, and beautiful.

How was she his?

"Think I'll go see what smells so good down there." Evan slipped past Bella and was down the stairs before Ben could form another thought.

Shaking himself, he closed the distance between them and dropped in for a kiss. "Hey, gorgeous. I missed you." Even though they worked together, he hated saying goodbye to her every night and thought fondly of the days she'd lived down the hall as a guest. But they'd both agreed that having their own space to retreat to was a healthy boundary for their new relationship, and she'd moved into the second bedroom of Shannon's condo upon returning to Walker Beach.

Absence did indeed make the heart grow fonder.

"Flattery will get you everywhere. Now, what are you doing up here standing around and chatting while I work my tail off down there?"

"Well, I'm the boss, so, naturally, I was supervising."

Her lips curved in a wry grin. They both knew who really ran this place. "Is that so?"

"Of course. And as the boss, I think you need to go back to work. What am I paying you for? To stand around and chat?" He mimicked her earlier tone.

Her eyes flashed with mirth. "Fine. I mean, I was going to tell you that everything is ready, and I had a little time to stand here in your arms and enjoy the fruits of our labor, but if you say I should go back to work, then yeah." She saluted. "You're the boss."

As she turned, he snagged her around the waist and tugged her to him. Her giggles warmed him all the way through. "Not so fast. I've reconsidered my directive." He settled her back against his chest, wrapping his arms around her shoulders.

She placed her hands over his and snuggled back into his embrace. "And what's the new one?"

Pressing his cheek against the side of Bella's head, he inhaled the intoxicating scent of her. "Stay." His lips lingered near her ear, grazing it when he spoke. "Never leave me."

"Your wish is my command."

And, still in his arms, Bella turned her head and captured his mouth in the same way she'd captured every part of him.

Oh man, he loved this woman. That indefinable thing had become definable.

And someday soon, he'd tell her.

For now, though, he would simply enjoy this moment, one that defined true success. And not because he'd saved the inn.

But because he'd finally trusted again—and had won everything in the gamble.

Want more? Access a bonus epilogue with just a bit more of Ben and Bella's happily ever after on my Reader Freebies page at www.lindsayharrel.com/reader-freebies.

CONNECT WITH LINDSAY

Thanks so much for joining Ben and Bella on their journey! I hope you loved them as much as I do. If so, would you mind doing me a favor and leaving a review on Goodreads, Bookbub, or your favorite retail site?

I'd love to connect with you. Sign up for my newsletter at www.lindsayharrel.com/subscribe and I'll send you a FREE story as a thank you!

Can't get enough of Walker Beach? You can read Evan's story in the next book, *All Because of You.* Turn the page for a sneak peek...

ALL BECAUSE OF YOU SNEAK PEEK

Two weeks. She only had to endure Walker Beach for two weeks.

Madison Price gripped the steering wheel as she parallel parked in front of the quaint blue and yellow storefront on Main Street. At first glance, Hole-in-the-Wall Hardware looked much the same as it always had.

But one thing was glaringly different from the last time she'd been here—Aunt Chrissy wasn't.

An ache pierced her heart, but Madison shook it away. She pulled her phone from her purse and shot off the text she'd considered sending during the entire four-hour drive north from Los Angeles. *I want to make an offer on the Dalton Street House. Asking price, like we discussed. Thanks.*

She hoped her realtor in Oregon would respond soon. Not that Madison didn't have plenty to distract her in the meantime. But it would be nice to have a home to go along with the assistant librarian job she'd start in just fifteen days.

Madison cast another wary glance at the store to her right, climbed from the packed-to-the-hilt car, and tucked her phone into the back pocket of her jeans. She probably should have dropped off her stuff at Aunt Chrissy's house, but something had compelled her to come here first. Dodging a few stray passersby, Madison unlocked the front door and stepped into the darkened store.

A small bit of light filtered in from the large front window, enough for her to make out the shadowed rows of hardware supplies and the hulking oak desk where she'd seen her aunt countless times, cashing out Walker Beach patrons and dishing out a larger-than-life smile. The place still smelled of wood dust and lemon, a mixture so familiar that she hadn't realized she'd missed it until now.

Madison reached for the light switch, but as she did, the back door creaked open and something clattered to the ground. Even from the front of the store, she could hear the wooden floorboards in the back groan and settle as someone walked across them.

Her breath stuttered. Was a thief taking advantage of the relatively quiet day on Main Street and the store that had been empty for more than four months? Walker Beach, California, had always been synonymous with safety, but a lot could have changed in the ten years since Madison had lived here.

Tiptoeing to the closest shelf where the hammers once had been stored, she fumbled along until she gripped a solid wooden handle. As quietly as she could, she crept toward the back, where someone was making quite a racket. If it were a thief, they were not a stealthy one.

After advancing through the front room, she tucked herself behind the desk and peered around the corner into the small kitchen that served as a break room. Her eyes first caught sight of the open back door and the sand and ocean just beyond. Then her gaze roamed the room, landing on a pair of legs. What the . . .

A man was lying on his back, his head stuck underneath the

break room sink, a wrench in his hand. And he was humming. Loudly.

OK, so most likely not a thief, unless there was some black-market demand for plumbing parts she didn't know about. But for some reason the heightened speed of her pulse continued. Madison stepped fully into the room. "What are you doing in my store?"

The man surged into a sitting position, his head smacking the top of the cabinet along the way. The wrench hurtled to the ground as he covered his face with his hands, groaning.

Sucking in a breath, Madison rushed forward. "Oh, sorry. I didn't mean for that to happen."

But at that moment, the man lowered his hand, and Madison couldn't help the gasp that fell from her lips.

What was *he* doing here?

Evan Walsh was as handsome now as he'd been during their senior year of high school. Instead of the tousled hair that had always made him appear as if he'd just rolled out of bed, he sported a casual blond brush-up. A defined jawline and full stubble had replaced sparse whiskers, and his wider shoulders gave way to crafted arms that peeked out from the rolled sleeves of his blue dress shirt. The only thing that hadn't changed about him were those piercing aqua eyes, the ones that had inspired more than one female at Walker Beach High to compose a silly love poem.

And yet, the sight of him still clenched Madison's stomach. "I asked what you're doing in my store."

"*Your* store?" He studied her for a moment, eyebrows puckered in confusion, until his eyes widened. "Oh, wow, you must be Madison."

He made it sound like he had no idea who she was. As if he hadn't spent months writing her pen pal letters that had ended up being a cruel joke. Evan Walsh, of all people, should have known her name.

Or maybe he only remembered the one he'd invented for her.

"Yeah, I'm Madison." *Not* Lizard Lady.

Evan stared at her, a grin curling around his lips. "And, Madison, tell me, what exactly are you planning to do with that?" His amused gaze traveled to her hand, and she looked down.

Instead of the hammer she'd intended to grab in defense, she'd snagged a plunger.

She set it down onto the small table behind her as her cheeks reddened. "I thought you were a thief."

"And so you said, 'Hey, I'll plunge the guy to death?'" Evan stood and brushed off his beige slacks, chuckling.

Madison backed up at his sudden nearness. "Well? Why are you here?"

"Your aunt asked me to keep an eye on things until you came back or sold the place. Of course, if I'd known it would be nearly five months, I'd have asked for double what she was paying me." At her lack of reply, he tilted his head, his smile disappearing. "Hey, it's just a joke. Are you OK?"

"Why would she have asked *you* for help?" Her aunt knew how Madison had felt about him and his dumb friends. Not that it mattered anymore.

Evan rubbed the back of his neck, a guarded look on his face. "We became close during the last few years." He cleared his throat. "I'm really sorry for your loss, by the way."

Heat flashed at the back of Madison's eyes, and she blinked rapidly before any tears could escape. "Thank you." Her voice nearly broke as she said the words.

Oh goodness. Air. She needed air.

Madison strode through the back door and onto the peeling wraparound porch. The breeze coming off the ocean attacked Madison's hair. From here, the wooden boardwalk that spanned the length of the town was only a stone's throw away. It wound like a slatted snake across the sparkling sands, where the Pacific whooshed in and out. Even on this Monday in early January, a handful of tourists and villagers walked the beach, enjoying the quiet landscape that was so different from the big cities of Los Angeles and San Francisco. Walker Beach was a few hundred miles from each and a world unto itself.

She may not have missed Walker Beach—or most of its people—but nothing could compete with this view.

"Hey."

Madison jumped and spun at the intrusion, fixing what she hoped was an intimidating glare on Evan, who now leaned against the doorjamb, hands tucked inside his pockets.

"I was just kidding about the five-months thing. I didn't mind helping out. I'm sure you've had a lot going on with school."

"How did you know about that?" She'd only just graduated three weeks ago, and life since then had been a whirlwind of packing her apartment and celebrating the holidays with her grandma in San Francisco.

"Chrissy told me." Evan shrugged. "She made it sound like you wouldn't want to keep the business or the house but knew it may help you out financially to sell them. I actually wasn't sure if you'd come yourself or just send movers to pack up everything."

Madison had considered it, but someone had to do Chrissy's things justice. Grandma hadn't wanted anything to do with Walker Beach since Grandpa had died. She hadn't even held Chrissy's funeral here.

So it was up to Madison, who had received the shock of her life when she'd been named heir of Chrissy's house and the hardware store that had been in the family for fifty years. It had taken her some time to work up her courage, but she was here now, with the perfect window of time before her dream job began. She'd get Chrissy's things sorted, her store inventoried, and her house and Hole-in-the-Wall Hardware on the market. Easy peasy.

But wait. Evan acted like . . . "So, you knew she was sick?" It wasn't something her aunt had shared with anyone in her family, including Madison. But perhaps she'd known that Madison would have abandoned her last year of school in a heartbeat if the word *cancer* had crossed her lips. It was the least she would have done for the woman who had taken in her twelve-year-old niece when Madison had lost her parents in a freak avalanche during a ski trip in Vermont.

Evan kicked at a rock on the patio. "Yeah."

"She didn't tell me." Madison swallowed hard. She should have been there. She should have known. If she'd bothered to come back to Walker Beach . . . But the town had held such painful memories—or so she'd told herself. Aunt Chrissy had come several times to visit Madison in Los Angeles, and Madison had counted that as enough.

But she'd left her aunt alone when she'd needed Madison most.

"I'm sorry."

Well, not completely alone. Apparently, Evan Walsh had been there.

Madison studied him, but no matter how hard she looked, he was an enigma. The expression in his eyes was clearly pained, but her pain and anger wouldn't let her embrace his. Chrissy had been Madison's aunt, and this was Madison's store. She didn't need Evan's help anymore.

She squared her shoulders. "I appreciate you keeping an eye on things, but I'm here now."

He nodded, quietly accepting her words, which had come out a bit harsher than she'd intended. "How long will you be here?" His question sounded nervous, though she couldn't imagine why it should.

"I'm not sure. There's a lot to do."

"Let me know if you need any help."

Help? From him? She'd sooner swim in the freezing-cold ocean and take a subsequent dip in a vat of ice. But she'd never let him know how much he'd wounded her in the past. It didn't matter anymore. She was over it, and she was better for it.

Madison jutted her chin forward. "I don't think I will, but thanks."

He eyed her for a moment. "Guess I'll go, then." Turning, he started down the cracked steps.

"Wait. Evan?"

"Yeah?" He circled back, and something in his eyes looked hopeful. But that was silly.

"I'll take your key."

"Oh. Right." Pulling the key from his pocket, his fingers brushed her palm as he handed it to her.

"Thanks." Madison rubbed away the fire that fanned from the spot where he'd touched her to the tips of her fingers.

They stared at each other until the ringing of her phone shattered the silence between them.

Madison pulled the phone from her back pocket, swiveled on her heel, and marched inside the store. She closed the back door in such haste that it slammed.

Why had she let the man rattle her so much? Or maybe it was simply being back here, in a place she couldn't help but love because of its previous owner. Yes, that had to be it. Evan Walsh was nothing to her. She needed to remember that.

The phone continued to blare. Oh, right. Without looking at the Caller ID, Madison clicked the green button on her screen. "Hello?"

"Is this Madison?"

"Yes. Who is this?" Madison slid into the nearest chair at the two-person table in the break room.

"Courtney Lambdon at Lola Public Library."

Her future boss. "Hi. How are you?"

"Not so great, actually. I hate to be the bearer of bad news, but the grant money we were planning to use to fund your position fell through. I'm afraid we can no longer offer you the job."

"What?" This had to be a sick joke. She'd already sublet her apartment in L.A., quit her job at the bookstore, packed. "There's nothing you can do?"

"I'm sorry, but no. We will, of course, search for other grant opportunities, but there is no guarantee we'll get one. If we do, I will let you know as soon as possible."

That wasn't good enough. She needed a job now. Maybe she could reach out to other libraries. She'd prefer to stay on the West Coast, but it didn't matter where, really. It wasn't like she had any real roots tying her down.

But that would take time and a bit of luck. She'd been lucky to find the job in Oregon.

Madison issued a weak thank you to Courtney and hung up the phone. Groaning, she rubbed her temples. What was she going to do now?

Her eyes caught sight of a sign hanging over the doorway: Follow Your Dreams. How many times had Aunt Chrissy told her that?

"Yeah, I tried, Aunt Chrissy. And look where it got me."

Back in the last place she wanted to be with nothing but a house and a store she'd never asked for.

BOOKS BY LINDSAY HARREL

Walker Beach Romance Series

All At Once (prequel novella)

All of You, Always

All Because of You

All I've Waited For

All You Need Is Love

Port Willis Series

The Secrets of Paper and Ink

Like a Winter Snow

Like a Christmas Dream

Standalones

The Joy of Falling

The Heart Between Us

One More Song to Sing

ABOUT THE AUTHOR

Lindsay Harrel is a lifelong book nerd who lives in Arizona with her young family and two golden retrievers in serious need of training. When she's not writing or chasing after her children, Lindsay enjoys making a fool of herself at Zumba, curling up with anything by Jane Austen, and savoring sour candy one piece at a time. Visit her at www.lindsayharrel.com.

facebook.com/lindsayharrel

instagram.com/lindsayharrelauthor

Walker Beach Romance Series

Book 1: All of You, Always

Published by Blue Aster Press

Cover: Hillary Manton Lodge Design

Editing: Marisa Deshaies

CPSIA information can be obtained
at www.ICGtesting.com
Printed in the USA
LVHW092037080421
683868LV00006B/1157